W9-CMF-648

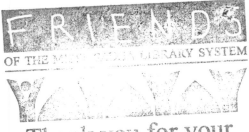

ZOM-B

ZOM-B
CLANS

DARREN
SHAN

HarperCollins*PublishersLtd*

For:
Conan Gorenstein
lost too soon
Even in death may he be triumphant!

OBE (Order of the Bloody Entrails) to:
Camilla Leask – clan PR

My clan of editors:
Venetia Gosling
Kate Sullivan
Elv Moody

Agents of the night:
the Christopher Little Agency

THEN . . .

When Becky Smith's racist father told her to throw an innocent black boy to a pack of zombies, she did it because she had spent her whole life obeying his orders. Instantly horrified by what she had done, she told her father that he was a monster and cut herself off from him. She was killed soon after and turned into one of the living dead. Unlike most of her kind, she regained the use of her brain, the result of a vaccine which had been given to her as a child by Dr Oystein, the world's first sentient zombie.

Desperate to atone for her crime in whatever small way she could, B joined Dr Oystein's Angels, teenagers like her who had pledged to fight for the future of the world's living survivors. It was to be a tense, terrible war. They not only faced the flood of brain-hungry zombies, there were other forces stacked against them, such as the sinister Mr Dowling and his mutants, the mysterious Owl Man, nightmarish babies and a powerful group of humans known as the Board, who tormented revitaliseds for fun.

After an uncertain start, and a period of captivity in which she was forced to fight for the amusement of the Board, B settled into life as an Angel, trained hard and developed swiftly. For her first proper mission, she and her room-mates were asked to escort a group of humans to New Kirkham, a town outside London. She hooked up with Vinyl along the way, an old friend of hers who had come through the attacks unscathed and was working with the Angels to try and restore order.

Having successfully delivered their group to New Kirkham, B and her team set off for their base in County Hall. But, as they were returning, B spotted Owl Man and a troop of humans dressed as members of the Ku Klux Klan. Though she had only her gut instinct to base it on, she was certain that they were heading for the town, and that Owl Man's primary aim in going there was to get hold of Vinyl. She had started to believe that Owl Man had been following her around London, and that he wished to use her friend to somehow manipulate her.

The other Angels were unconvinced by B's arguments, but agreed to retrace their footsteps, to make sure everything was OK. To their dismay, they found the robed vigilantes rounding up anyone who wasn't white or British. They were assisted by some of the settlement's residents, who had welcomed the Klan with open arms — in fact, a number of them had been secretly working with the KKK in advance, and they were the ones who had let in the savage invaders.

Some of the townsfolk had fought back, but most stood by neutrally, letting events play out, abandoning people who had previously been their friends and allies. It seemed, in this horrific world of the living dead, that most of the survivors were more interested in saving themselves than in fighting for those who needed their help.

B and her fellow Angels didn't do neutral. Without a thought for their own safety, they scaled the wall, slipped into town unseen, moved in on the racist tormentors and attacked.

NOW . . .

ONE

The Klanners drove to New Kirkham in jeeps, vans and trucks, which they parked in the town's main square. While many of them rampage through the streets, on the hunt for anyone they don't approve of, the rest force their prisoners into cages and load them up. They cackle as they work, beating their captives, firing shots into the air, whooping wildly. They've already notched up plenty of murders, and corpses lie strewn across the ground.

Owl Man is grimly overseeing it all from the back of a jeep. He's a strange-looking figure. He has enormous eyes, all white except for a dark dot at the centre of each, a thin frame and a pot belly, white hair and long, creepy fingers. He dresses in a striped suit with a pink shirt.

Owl Man is studying his pet dog as it roots among the guts of a guy it killed moments before. The dog looks like an ordinary sheepdog, but when it opens its mouth, it has fangs like a zombie's, and bones slide from its claws when it attacks. Owl Man called the dog Sakarias.

'Clever doggie,' Owl Man murmurs as Sakarias rips the dead man's heart from his chest, tosses it high into the air, catches it and wolfs it down. Then he hears my war cry as I charge into the square, the rest of my crew behind me. He looks up and smiles. 'Ah,' he says in his smooth voice, sounding pleased. 'The undead cavalry comes riding to the rescue. This should be interesting.'

Ignoring Owl Man, we tear into the startled members of the Ku Klux Klan and the men and women of New Kirkham who have been helping them.

Ashtat's hands and feet are a blur as she unleashes

one perfectly orchestrated karate chop after another. She was worried that she might not be able to bring herself to kill a living human, no matter how evil they might be. She needn't have been concerned. She's like a biblical warrior angel, raining down hellfire on anyone who gets in her way.

Pearse and Conall flank her, picking off anyone she misses. The ginger-haired pair have more first-hand experience of battle than the rest of us, but I'm sure they've never had to deal with a situation like this before.

Carl leaps around like a crazy killer frog and strikes swiftly every time he lands. The speedy Jakob races after Carl, backing him up, targeting those who scatter ahead of the acrobatic teenager.

Shane and I wade into those standing close to the trucks, throwing one jab after another, ripping open throats, breaking bones, crushing skulls.

That last bit is crucial. All hell is breaking loose, but each one of us takes the time to crack open the skull of every person we kill, destroying the brain inside. Otherwise the corpses would revive and attack the humans, causing even more problems than the Klanners.

The humans in hoods fly into a panic. They weren't expecting an attack of this nature. Most of them have guns. If they closed ranks and worked as a team, they could pick us off easily. But they're all over the place. They wheel away from one another, firing crazily, screaming, jumping at shadows. It's utter chaos, which suits us perfectly.

The dog became alert as soon as it heard my challenging roar. Looking up from its meal, it glanced around, took in everything that was happening, identified the various threats, then hurled itself at Carl, who was its nearest target.

Sakarias chases after the springing Carl. It snaps at his heels and just misses as he soars overhead. As it turns to follow him, Jakob grabs it by the scruff of its neck and tries to wrestle it to the ground. The dog shrugs him off – it must be a lot stronger than it looks – then locks its jaws round his left arm. Jakob screams as it chews through his flesh and bone, shaking its head, trying to rip the arm free of its socket.

'Sakarias!' Owl Man calls, then whistles sharply. The dog instantly releases Jakob and bounds back to its master, leaving a relieved Jakob to grit his teeth against the pain – we don't feel it as much as the living, but serious wounds definitely hurt – and rejoin the action.

I grab a Klanner – a short, thin, wiry woman – and smash her head open against the side of a truck. Turning from her corpse, I fix on Owl Man and start towards him. The dog spots me and draws to a halt ahead of the jeep where its master is standing. It squares up to me, snarling, blood dripping from its fangs, the fur around its face soaked with the red stuff and covered in scraps of gut, sharp bones jutting out of the tips of all its paws.

'Easy, Sakarias,' Owl Man purrs, studying me with an amused look.

I take the dog's measure and decide I don't fancy the fight. I spot a discarded gun and pick it up. Dr Oystein and Master Zhang abhor guns. They've trained us to fight without them, told us never to resort to using such foul weapons. But in my book there's a time and a place for everything. Steadying my arm, I aim at the mutant dog's face.

'No,' Owl Man barks, his smile vanishing. 'Drop it.'

I sneer and start to hurl an insult at him. Then I stare with astonishment as my fingers open and the gun falls. Confused, I bend to retrieve it.

'Leave it alone, Becky,' Owl Man mutters, and for some sickening reason I stop short of picking it up. 'Kneel,' Owl Man whispers, and I find myself obeying his soft command.

As I stare at Owl Man with shock and terror, he climbs down from the jeep and strolls towards me, clicking his tongue for the dog to follow. The pair stop in front of me and Owl Man sears me with his unnatural gaze.

'Little girls should not play with guns,' he growls. 'You have betrayed the wishes of your superiors. You should be ashamed of yourself.'

'How ... are you ... doing this?' I snarl, willing myself to attack him, but unable to get my limbs to respond.

'Oh, I'm a man of many subtle talents,' Owl Man says with a wicked chuckle. He walks around me, then whistles again at the dog and makes a gesture with his left hand. Sakarias opens its mouth wide and fastens its fangs round my throat. I moan and stare at the sky, expecting it to be the last thing I see before the dog severs my head and digs into my brain.

'If you ever threaten Sakarias again, I will tell him to finish you off,' Owl Man says. 'He is a sweet animal who only kills when ordered or if we are threatened. Those of us with a choice must be kind to the dumb creatures of the world. Otherwise we are no better than the reviveds who tear their heads open for the sweet brains within.'

Owl Man clicks his fingers and Sakarias withdraws. The dog gives me an evil look, then follows its master back to the jeep, where the pair hop onboard.

'Your body is your own again,' Owl Man says with a mocking smile. To my relief, I find myself in control once more. Flexing my fingers, I get to my feet and shake my arms and legs. I feel like my heart is beating fast, but that was ripped from my chest when I was turned into a zombie, so I know it's my imagination.

'What the hell happened?' Shane shouts, pulling up beside me.

'I don't know,' I croak, then cock my head at him. 'Where were you?'

'Back there,' he says.

'Why didn't you help me?'

He looks sheepish. 'I couldn't move.'

'Owl Man was controlling you too?' I ask sympathetically.

He grins shakily. 'Not exactly. I was just too stunned to do anything.'

I roll my eyes and curse him, then look around to see how the battle is going. It seems to be favouring us. About a hundred of the white citizens of New Kirkham took a stand against the Klan when they invaded. They were led by the mayor, Biddy Barry. The Klan had the rebels clustered against a wall when we attacked, but now they've overthrown their captors and massed behind us. With Biddy's roaring encouragement, the men and women grab weapons and throw themselves into combat with their racist foes.

Some of the prisoners have broken free from their cages and holding pens, but many are still under lock and key. A few of the sharper drivers see that they're fighting a lost cause. Showing little concern for their colleagues, three of them start their trucks and roar towards the main road out of the square. Owl Man bangs on the side of his jeep and his driver fires up the engine and tears after them.

I don't want to let Owl Man escape. I'm still furious about the way he turned me into a puppet. I want to pay him back, catch up with the jeep, take him by surprise and strike before he can say a word. But I can't abandon the people of New Kirkham. They need our help. I decide to stand my ground.

Then, just as I've made up my mind to stay, I spot cages in one of the trucks, filled with humans. The prisoners are screaming, weeping, tugging at the bars. If I was right about Owl Man coming here for Vinyl, it's a sure bet that he was one of the first they caged and loaded up, that he's almost certainly among those in one of the three fleeing trucks.

I glance around again. Biddy Barry and her troops seem to have things in hand. It won't be easy, but with the aid of the Angels they should triumph. But nobody is thinking about the people on the trucks. If I don't try to do something now, the Klanners will escape with dozens – if not more – of the townsfolk.

'Stay here and oversee things,' I bark at Shane. 'I'm guessing that lots of the Klan are scattered around the town, still searching for victims. Organise a hunt for them once you're done with this lot.'

'Are you going after the trucks?' Shane asks.

'Yeah. And the guy with the eyes. I want him too.'

He shudders. 'Rather you than me.'

'That's why I'm a badass and you're a wuss,' I laugh. Then I sprint after the jeep and trucks, murder most horrid on my mind.

TWO

I hurry through the town, chasing the sounds of the trucks and jeep. I won't be able to keep up with them if they make it out of New Kirkham and into the open, but on these streets, being able to take shortcuts up alleys while they have to follow the road and go slow round corners, I start to catch up.

I pass a few stray Klanners. Some take potshots at me. Others cower and beg for mercy. I ignore them all, leaving them for the others to deal with.

I'm slipping past what used to be a fish and chip shop when there's a thump behind me. I think it's some sort of missile, so I hurl myself aside and cover my head with my hands.

'What are you doing?' an amused voice asks.

I look up to find Carl Clay standing over me. Jakob is running after him.

'Don't you know it's rude to sneak up on a girl?' I snap, uncurling myself.

'We saw you quitting the party early,' Carl grins. 'Figured you might need backup.'

'But we'll be happy to leave you to your own devices if you prefer,' Jakob adds as he arrives, wincing with pain.

Carl is handsome and sleekly groomed, always sporting the finest designer gear. Jakob looks like he's a centimetre shy of death's door and usually wears baggy clothes to disguise his skeletal, cancer-ridden frame. They're an odd couple, but they match each other in a weird, undead kind of way.

'My first priority is to free the prisoners in the trucks,' I tell them. 'But I want to kill Owl Man too, if I can sneak up on him and strike before he opens his mouth. Did you see him perform his Jedi mind trick on me?'

'What are you talking about?' Carl frowns.

'Never mind. There's no time to explain. Just don't confront him head-on. Hit him from behind, when he's not looking, and don't let him speak.'

'That's not very chivalrous,' Carl sniffs.

'Screw chivalry,' I snarl.

We press on after the vehicles. I soon find myself falling behind. Carl leaps ahead of us and Jakob swiftly outpaces me. I don't mind. This isn't about personal glory. It's about getting the job done.

I try not to think about how Owl Man took control of my body. It was terrifying at the time, but even more so looking back. It makes me wonder what else he could force me to do, and when. I mean, if he can manipulate me up close, can he do it from afar as well, any time he likes?

The noise of the trucks and jeep alters and comes closer. That confuses me for a moment. Then I realise they must have hit a dead end and been forced to turn. They don't know this town. They're intruders, fish out of water.

I spot the vehicles rumbling past at the end of the street. Carl and Jakob have paused and shifted to the sides to hide themselves from view. I'm too far away to have to worry, though I could swear that Owl Man's head turns as they pass, that he looks my way and smirks.

Carl and Jakob wait for me to join them, then the three of us gaze after the diminished remains of the convoy. Members of the Klan are clinging to the sides of the truck at the rear. The back doors are open. We can see cages inside, people locked up, still banging on the bars and screaming for help.

'I'm going to target that one,' Carl says, squatting and tensing his legs, getting ready to spring. 'I'll leave the other trucks and Owl Man to you guys.'

'We should stick together,' I mutter.

He shakes his head. 'If we can take a truck each, we might be able to save everyone.'

'And Owl Man?' I ask.

Carl shrugs. 'He's got to be a bonus, nothing more.

If he gets away, so be it. The prisoners have to come first.'

Before I can finish processing that and tell Carl that I think he's right, he's gone, springing forward like a grasshopper. He lands close to the truck, then propels himself into the air again. This time he comes down on the roof. He almost slides off, but digs in with his fingerbones and starts crawling towards the cab at the front.

Jakob and I resume our pursuit of the remaining trucks, but he stays by my side now, reining himself in. As we chase the vehicles, the truck that Carl landed on swerves, then crashes into a building. The humans clinging to the sides are crushed or shaken loose. As we storm past, we spot Carl emerging from the driver's cab. He lays into those who survived the crash, cutting them down before they can flee, moving towards the opening at the back to free the prisoners.

'Give them hell, Carl!' I whoop, and he waves a hand to acknowledge me. Then we move on and the chase continues.

THREE

I have the remaining three vehicles in sight – the jeep is in front of the two trucks now, having overtaken them along the way – when they suddenly swerve out of view. Jakob and I get to the corner and turn after them, then draw to a sickened halt.

We're close to one of the town's perimeter walls. There's a large gate ahead of us. It's like the one we saw when we first came here, designed to open and close swiftly. Owl Man or one of the Klanners must have been in contact with the operators of the gate, issuing instructions as they were getting close, because a handful of humans are racing towards the trucks, while behind them the gate has been opened and zombies are starting to stream through.

Jakob and I stare at the open gate and the inrushing reviveds, then at each other.

'This is bad,' Jakob whispers.

'No,' I correct him. 'This is terrible.'

The jeep slows and lets the trucks overtake it. They hit the zombies at the front of the invading hordes and plough through them, clearing a path for the less heavyweight jeep. The drivers have to slow down, but they maintain a steady crawl. Those who fall beneath the trucks erupt seconds later in geysers of blood. There must be some sort of machine attached to the underbellies of the vehicles.

The Klanners inside the trucks pull in their associates who opened the gates, then slam the doors shut on the zombies, settling back to leave the hard work to the drivers.

'We've got to close the gate,' Jakob says. 'Stop the stream of reviveds before it's too late.'

I nod numbly, then study the distance between

myself and the wall. I look at the trucks and jeep again and try to calculate how long it's going to take them to clear the mob of zombies.

'Can you manage by yourself?' I ask.

Jakob squints at me. 'You have somewhere else you'd rather be?'

'I can't give up on the people in the trucks,' I groan. 'I have to try and save them.'

'By yourself?' Jakob asks sceptically.

I nod glumly. 'I know it's crazy, but once they clear that wall the drivers will have an open road ahead of them. I don't fancy my chances, but I'm the only hope they have. Even if I can't stop both trucks, maybe I can force at least one of them to crash.'

Jakob shakes his head. 'I don't know if you're incredibly brave or unbelievably stupid.'

'There's no question about that,' I laugh sickly. 'Stupid, for sure.'

'What about the one with the large eyes?' Jakob asks.

'I can't worry about him now. All I can do is focus

on the trucks, try to stop them and hope I can catch up with Owl Man later.'

Jakob smiles. 'I should probably try to stop you, but who am I to stand in the way of a would-be hero? Good luck, B. If I don't see you again, I just want you to know you were always a pain in the arse.'

'Eat me,' I retort with my own shaky smile.

Jakob sets off at top speed. I veer towards the wall and pump my legs as hard as I can. Some of the zombies lumber after me, thinking I'm one of the living, but I've a good start on them and they don't cause me any concern.

This is madness. It would be tough enough if it was just me against all the Klanners in the trucks, but Owl Man has shown he can literally bend me to his will. All he has to do is tell me to freeze and I'll be helpless to protect myself. I could try to take him by surprise and knock him out before he can work his voodoo magic, but then the trucks might get away while I'm dealing with him.

'Sod it,' I tell myself. 'I'll cross that chasm of hellfire when I come to it. First things first.'

31

I get to the wall and climb a rope ladder. One of the trucks is passing through the gate, the jeep and the other vehicle not far behind. I start running again, along the path that follows the top of the wall.

You're not really going to do this, are you? the sensible part of me protests as a rough plan forms inside my head.

'You betcha, baby!' I cackle.

You're nuts, I tell myself in disgust.

'I know you are,' I retort childishly.

Then I come to a platform above the gate and, as the second truck is grinding its way through the zombies packed tight into the space, I make a sharp turn and leap over the barbed wire which runs round the perimeter. I clear the wire, along with the end of the wall, and hurtle towards the roof of the leading truck.

Arms flailing, I hit the roof and bounce towards the edge. I was sure I'd slide off – my plan was to get up and chase the truck once I'd landed – but to my surprise I manage to dig in my fingerbones and hold on. If the driver notices, he doesn't pay any attention to me, picking up speed once he's clear of the gate, powering ahead, leaving the zombies behind.

I'm tossed around like a rag doll, barely clinging on to the roof, legs hanging over the side. I try hauling myself up but I can't. It's taking everything I have just to hold on. I think about releasing my grip and following on foot, like I originally planned, but the vehicles are moving quickly now that they're on the open road. I wouldn't be able to keep up.

The mad ride lasts no more than four or five minutes, but it feels like hours, and my arms are screaming from the strain. Then we crest a hill and glide out of sight of New Kirkham and the zombies. We carry on for a few hundred metres, then the truck draws to a halt, tyres squealing. Dust flies up into the air and I go flying forward, unable to stop myself.

I hit the ground hard and cry out as I roll across the road. My eyes shake in their sockets and the world becomes a white, hazy cloud.

I hear the truck trundling towards me — if the driver wasn't aware of me before, he knows all about me now. I try backing away from it, but I can't get to my feet, I'm still too shaken from the ride and the fall.

The truck comes closer. My eyes start to clear. I see that the front of the truck is above me. My legs are beneath the bumper. I spot loads of blades attached to the chassis. Seems I was wrong about a machine. They don't need one. This is simpler and more effective.

The engine roars as the truck inches forward. The driver is toying with me, waiting for me to squirm and retreat. I won't give him the satisfaction. Since it's clearly a hopeless situation, I flip him the finger and hold my ground.

The engine roars again. The truck shudders forward a few centimetres. I brace myself for the end.

But then it stops. Not the noise – that's louder than ever – but the driver holds the truck where it is, threatening annihilation but not following through. I don't know why he's waiting. Maybe he wants to check with Owl Man first.

Then, as I lie pinned beneath the truck, one thrust

of the throttle away from death, the passenger door opens and somebody steps down.

'Fee-fi-fo-fith,' a man sings, 'I smell the blood of Becky Smith. And it smells *goooooooooood*!'

I recognise the voice. I also recognise the sailor's outfit as he steps into view. So, by the time he reveals his chubby, beaming face, I've recovered from my initial shock and am ready for him.

'Hello, Dan-Dan,' I sneer. 'Have you come out to play?'

FOUR

Daniel Wood was a member of the Board, the fat cats on HMS *Belfast* who held me prisoner and forced me to fight for their amusement. Billionaires, a prince, a racist MP. A powerful, nasty, self-centred lot, every one of them a true, rotten son or daughter of a bitch.

But Dan-Dan was the worst of them. Clearly psychotic, he kept a group of children on the cruiser to torment, torture and kill as he saw fit. He loved dressing up in ill-fitting suits that showed off his bulging, hairy belly, but the sailor's outfit was his favourite. He wore that more than any other.

'Hello, dear child,' Dan-Dan beams. 'What a joy to cross paths with you again. I was afraid I might not be able to make good on my parting promise. Do you remember that, my sweet little undead girl?'

'Sure. You wanted to pinch my cheek and kiss me goodnight.' I pucker up and let him see my fangs. 'Come on then, fat boy, I'm ready and waiting.'

'Isn't she marvellous?' Dan-Dan says to one of the two armed guards who got out behind him. They're packing menacing-looking rifles, ready to cut me down if I wriggle free and attack. To my surprise, the guard he addresses is familiar to me.

'Lovely to see you again, Coley,' I say sarcastically.

The guard with short hair and designer sunglasses flashes me an evil grin. 'The pleasure is all mine.'

Coley used to be the partner of an ex-soldier called Barnes. They worked for the Board. Barnes had a change of heart and helped set me free. Coley wasn't similarly inclined, so Barnes tied him up and left him somewhere. Looks like he went back and cut Coley's bonds as planned after he'd freed me. Coley must have then found his way back to one of his old masters, and was now serving as he had before.

'So Zombies didn't get to you before Barnes untied you?' I ask sweetly.

Coley scowls. 'Don't mention that bastard's name around me.'

'Such a shame when good friends fall out,' I chuckle viciously, then focus on Dan-Dan again. 'Why don't you ditch the guards and face me by yourself, fatso?'

'Oh, I wouldn't dare,' he simpers. 'I know how fast and vicious you are. I'm a delicate flower. I wouldn't stand a chance if they left me to face you on my own.'

'You're a coward,' I snarl.

'Not at all,' he protests. 'I'm simply a pragmatist. What is money for, if not to surround yourself with people who can fight your battles for you? I'm many dreadful things, Becky Smith, but not a fighter. I know my limits.'

Dan-Dan shifts around, studying me from different angles. He frowns. 'You look fresher than the last time I saw you.'

'The result of a dip in a Groove Tube, I imagine,' Owl Man says, appearing behind the fake sailor. Sakarias is at his heel. With its mouth closed, it looks like an ordinary, friendly sheepdog. I instinctively want to reach out and pat it.

'What's a Groove Tube?' Dan-Dan asks.

'I will explain later,' Owl Man says. He stares at me sternly, the way some of my teachers used to when I failed to hand in homework on time. 'You should not have followed us, Becky.'

'It's B, numbnuts,' I growl. 'At least get my name right if you're gonna kill me.'

'I was never one for nicknames or abbreviations,' he says, then smiles. 'Which makes your owlish name for me all the more ironic.'

'How do you know about that?' I ask.

'I know all sorts of things about you,' Owl Man says. 'I have been keeping a close watch on you since we first met in your home all those months ago.'

'Then I was right about you following me,' I growl. 'The others didn't believe me, but when I saw that dog a few times, I knew it couldn't be coincidence.'

'Indeed not,' Owl Man smiles.

'You know my Becky?' Dan-Dan is startled by the news.

'The pair of us go way back,' Owl Man murmurs.

'How extraordinary.' Dan-Dan scratches his stomach. 'Will you miss her as much as I'm going to once we kill her?'

'I will indeed miss her if she is taken from us,' Owl Man nods. 'But that will not be today. We must let her go.'

'What?' Dan-Dan barks, his smile vanishing.

'There will be another time for Becky Smith,' Owl Man says. 'For now, please ask your driver to back up. I will make sure she does not assault you.'

Dan-Dan glowers at Owl Man. 'You're out of your mind if you think I'm letting this savage minx waltz free. She killed my brother.'

'After you threw him to me,' I cheerfully remind him.

'Granted,' he says with a tilt of his head. 'But a family grievance cannot be forgotten so readily. She must pay for what she did to Luca. Besides,' he adds with a giggle, 'I've been *so* looking forward to this. I won't have as much time to toy with her as I would have liked, but I can work swiftly when I have to.'

'I asked you to *please* instruct your driver to back up,' Owl Man says, and although he speaks politely, there's no mistaking the menace in his tone. 'You will be doing me a favour if you set her free.'

Dan-Dan takes stock of his eerie-looking ally. 'I'm a man who knows the value of a favour,' he says carefully. 'I wouldn't reject you if I didn't have good cause. But this girl is mine. I've claimed her.'

'She was mine before she was yours,' Owl Man demurs.

'Screw the both of you!' I roar. 'I'm my own person.'

The two men ignore me. Their gazes are locked.

'If you cross me on this, I will be forced to withdraw my support for your various activities,' Dan-Dan says sweetly and, although I've no idea what they're talking about, I can see that his words have a big impact on Owl Man. 'I will urge Justin to

cancel his backing for you too and, as you know, Justin and I agree on most major issues.'

Owl Man's lips grow thin as he reacts poorly to the threat. 'I am a dangerous enemy,' he whispers.

'I'm all too aware of that,' Dan-Dan nods. 'I'm hoping that we can remain on friendly, mutually productive terms. But if alienating you is the cost of having my way in this matter, it's a cost I'm prepared to pay. I want her.' A dark shadow flits across his face. 'I *need* her.'

Owl Man sighs and strokes his dog's ears. 'Lack of self-control is a weakness, Daniel. You should strive to master your urges.'

'I control myself impeccably,' Dan-Dan sniffs. 'I just don't believe in not doing what I want. Life's too short to live by other people's rules. Coley understands what I mean, don't you, Coley?'

'One hundred per cent, my lord,' the guard growls.

'I must have the girl,' Dan-Dan continues. 'For me, at this moment, nothing else matters. I could drop dead of a heart attack on our way back to

London. If I do, I will die satisfied at having done all that I wanted while alive, not bitter because I let an opportunity pass.'

Owl Man smiles thinly. 'You are a troubled soul, my friend.'

'Yes,' Dan-Dan says. 'But I know how to make the troubles go away — by enjoying all of the freedoms which are rightfully mine.'

Owl Man considers the situation. He casts a worried look in my direction. I give him the finger and he tuts.

'The girl is important to me,' he tries one last time. 'She matters to Mr Dowling too. He will be unhappy if you harm her. This is not a wise move.'

'Look deep into my eyes,' Dan-Dan giggles. 'If you find the slightest trace of wisdom in them, do let me know.'

Owl Man hesitates a moment longer, then hardens his expression. 'So be it. We will deal with the fallout as best we can. But if you are going to kill her, do so quickly. We do not have time to stand around and play games.'

'Oh, there's always time for games,' Dan-Dan purrs as he heads back to the driver's cab. His guards keep their weapons trained on me. 'Now, will I start with knives and a saw, or should I build up to –'

A figure drops from the roof of the truck. There's a scuffling noise. Dan-Dan yelps. The guards whirl. Sakarias barks. Owl Man blinks.

Then Dan-Dan is dragged back into view by a massive teenager with short hair, small eyes and chubby cheeks. He has Dan-Dan in the mother of all headlocks and seems completely unfazed by the rifles that have been trained on him.

'Hey, Becky, I bet you never thought you'd be glad to see *me*,' says a wickedly grinning Rage.

FIVE

Rage ended up stranded outside the perimeter walls while the rest of us snuck into New Kirkham. I hadn't thought about him since we'd parted company. I certainly hadn't expected to come across him again like this.

'What the hell are you doing here, you great big ugly, beautiful beast?' I cry.

Rage grins. 'That's the sweetest thing you've ever said to me.'

'Let me go!' Dan-Dan bellows, kicking out at his captor. 'Shoot him!' he screams at the guards.

'Careful, big guy,' Rage laughs. 'One nick from me and you're history.'

Dan-Dan stops struggling. 'You're a zombie?' he moans.

'A revitalised,' Rage corrects him. 'That's why your guys haven't opened fire. If a few drops of my blood spatter you, you'll be munching brains for dessert tonight.'

'Coley?' Dan-Dan croaks. 'Is he telling the truth?'

'Yes,' Coley says and I can see that he's seething. He never did like it when things didn't go his way.

'Well, that's a real kick in the teeth,' Dan-Dan huffs. 'How did you sneak up on us like that, you clever boy?'

Rage frowns. 'You don't sound too petrified.'

'I accept the fact that I'll have to die one day, but I doubt it will be today,' Dan-Dan says chirpily. 'It would be different if we were alone, but you know that if you infect me, my guards will execute you on the spot. Your girlfriend too.'

'Girlfriend?' Rage snorts. 'You're way off the mark.'

'Then why risk so much to save her?' Dan-Dan asks.

'Yeah,' I say, shuffling out from under the truck. 'What gives? Where did you pop out of? And why put your life on the line? You don't care about me.'

Rage pretends to look sorrowful. 'Oh, the ingratitude. Didn't I come to your rescue on the *Belfast* too?'

'That was different. You tagged along because the odds were in our favour and you wanted to get in on the action.'

Rage laughs. 'I can't deny it. Although, in your position, I wouldn't be so quick to reveal all that to this lot. We should be putting on a show of unity, let them think we believe in that all-for-one crap.'

I curse beneath my breath. The most annoying thing about Rage is that he's right so much of the time. 'Just tell me how you got here,' I snarl.

He shrugs. 'It's hardly an epic story. I waited outside for the rest of you. I heard all the commotion and was gutted I couldn't be involved. Then I saw the trucks leaving and spotted you on top of one. I followed, keeping back so that I couldn't be seen. Well, obviously I *could* have been seen, but I figured their attention would be focused on the zombie clinging to the roof. I slipped up behind the trucks while Sinbad here was chatting with you. Waited for my moment. And here I am.'

'Some of your team should have been keeping watch, Coley,' Dan-Dan tuts.

'Normally we would have had several lookouts in place,' Coley grunts, his cheeks reddening. 'But the last few minutes have been crazy. In the chaos and confusion, our standards slipped. My apologies, sir. It won't happen again.'

'Assuming I let you live to command another day,' Dan-Dan says pointedly.

I edge over beside Rage and his prisoner. Nobody tries to stop me. Owl Man is studying us with an indecipherable expression. 'What now?' I mutter.

'We back off slowly and let these guys go on their merry way,' Rage says.

'You think they won't shoot us?'

'Not as long as I keep the Captain here under lock and key.'

'You really shouldn't make jokes about my costume,' Dan-Dan says. 'It's rude and insensitive.'

'Like I care,' Rage laughs and starts to back away.

'Hold it,' Coley barks. 'You're going nowhere until you release Lord Wood.'

Rage pauses and cocks an eyebrow at me. 'This guy's Daniel Wood? Why didn't you tell me?'

'I didn't think you'd have heard of him.'

'Are you kidding? He was infamous. The newspapers called him the Child Catcher. Nobody could ever make charges stick because he operated in out-of-the-way countries where judges and the police could be bribed.'

'They could be bribed in less out-of-the-way places too,' Dan-Dan chortles. 'I travelled more freely than the media reported.'

'I'm impressed,' Rage says. 'You're a celebrity. I must get your autograph before we go.'

'No one's going anywhere until you release Lord Wood,' Coley says again, pushing up his sunglasses to glare at us.

'Don't be stupid,' Rage says. 'I'm not gonna do

that. You'd shoot me before I made it to the brow of the hill.'

'I can't let you leave with him,' Coley retorts. 'You'd kill him once you were out of sight.'

'What if I promise to set him free and cross my heart and hope to die?' Rage smiles.

Coley shakes his head and returns the smile. 'You're already dead.'

'Then it looks like we have a problem.'

I stare at Rage. 'Surely you have a plan. You can't have just charged in and risked everything without thinking it through.'

He grins sheepishly.

'You should have left me to the racists,' I groan. 'At least then they wouldn't have known we were bloody amateurs.'

'If I may make a suggestion,' Owl Man intercedes and all eyes settle on him. 'We have Becky's friend, Vinyl, in one of the trucks.'

'So it *was* Vinyl you were after!' I shout.

Owl Man raises an eyebrow. 'You guessed that he was my focus?'

'The second I saw you on the road, when you were travelling here.'

He smiles. 'We are getting to know so much about one another, as good friends or enemies always do.'

'You let me see you on your way to New Kirkham,' I accuse him. 'You sent the dog to lure me in. You wanted me to come after you.'

Owl Man spreads his hands. 'Guilty as charged.'

'Why?'

He shrugs. 'To see what you would do. Most of your friends perished in the first wave of zombie attacks. I lost track of any who survived. When I saw Vinyl with you in Hammersmith, I figured he might be a useful bargaining chip further down the line. But first I needed to find out if you would risk everything to save him, so I called up the boys in the hoods — I've had them on standby for months now, for something like this.'

'You never told me about that,' Dan-Dan says petulantly.

'I do not share everything with my associates,' Owl Man says. 'Especially those who cross me where the undead are concerned. You should not have done that, Daniel. This is my field of expertise. My wishes should have been respected.'

'It was a conflict of interests,' Dan-Dan says. 'To you she's a zombie, to me she's a plaything. We had to clash sooner or later. I won't hold it against you.'

'He takes setbacks so manfully, doesn't he?' Owl Man says to me. Then he purses his lips thoughtfully. 'You can have Daniel. We will take Vinyl. When you return to London, bring Daniel to us and I will arrange a swap. We can iron out the finer details then.'

'Wait a minute,' Dan-Dan squawks, losing his cool. 'You can't leave me in the clutches of these foul brutes.'

'We have no choice,' Owl Man says. 'If you had let Becky go, as I asked, this could have been avoided. As things stand . . .'

'But they'll kill me!' Dan-Dan roars.

'No,' Owl Man says. 'Vinyl is one of Becky's oldest, dearest friends. She came back to save him. She will not harm you if she knows that she can swap you for him later.'

'What about the others?' I ask. 'They're just as important to me.'

'Are they really?' Owl Man looks sceptical.

'I wasn't sure that you had Vinyl,' I tell him. 'I chased after the trucks to try to help the people in the cages.'

Owl Man sighs. 'You have changed in so many ways. I am proud of what you have become. I wish I could care as much about people as you do.' He thinks about it for a moment. 'I can make no promises, since there are lots of different factors involved, but I give you my word that I will do my best to have them returned along with Vinyl, assuming you are happy to restore Lord Wood to us.'

'You expect me to trust you?' I snort.

'What other option do you have?' Owl Man says sweetly, then turns his back on us and calls his dog. 'Come, Sakarias, the jeep awaits. Mr Coley, will you and your people get back in your trucks and escort us?'

'Boss?' Coley asks uncertainly.

Dan-Dan sighs. 'Is there any other way we can resolve this?'

Coley licks his lips and thinks about it, then spits with disgust. 'Not that I can see.'

'Then we'll have to hope he knows what he's doing. If the girl hasn't delivered me to you within seventy-two hours, kill the boy slowly and painfully, along with everyone else from this rat's nest of a town. Now get the hell out of here so that this dratted beast can release me. I have a terrible crick in my neck.'

The guards and Owl Man mount up and set off. I hate having to stand here helplessly, but given the way things turned out, we've pushed this as far as we can. To be honest, I'm amazed we've got away with this much. Best not to ride our luck any further.

As the trucks trundle away, Rage gives Dan-Dan some space, but holds on to him, using him as a shield in case there are any long-range snipers onboard.

'Thanks,' I tell Rage softly. 'You didn't have to do this.'

'I know,' he sniffs. 'But what a kick! To take on

those guys and force a stand-off . . .' He punches the air. 'That's the most fun I've had in an age.'

'You'll regret it in the end,' Dan-Dan says. 'Anyone who has ever annoyed me has lived to wish they'd given me a wide berth.'

'Maybe,' Rage laughs. 'But I'm like you, Dan-Dan. I believe in living for the moment. We could all be worm food tomorrow, so we've got to make corn today.'

'It's make hay,' I correct him.

'Whatever.'

Dan-Dan stares at Rage. 'You remind me of myself when I was younger. If I get out of this mess, maybe I'll let you live. The world's a more interesting place with people of our calibre in it to add spice to the mix.'

'I'm welling up at the compliment,' Rage chuckles.

Dan-Dan's gaze turns my way and his eyes narrow. 'As you know, young man, I'm fabulously wealthy. I can give you anything you want. From what Becky said, there's no love lost between you, and you didn't seem to care much about the others on the trucks. Name your price for my freedom and the girl.'

Rage mulls it over and studies me coldly. I stand firm and get ready to fight. Then he grins and I relax.

'Sorry, Lord Wood,' he says, 'but I don't think you could match my price.'

'You don't know until you ask,' Dan-Dan gurgles.

'True,' Rage smirks. 'But luckily for Becky, I'm not in an asking mood.' He flashes his teeth at me. 'At least not today. Try me again later if she gets on my nerves.'

'Some hero,' I growl, but although I try to maintain an offended expression, I can't, and soon I'm smiling like a cat who's used up all nine of her lives only to be given yet one more. Stepping into line with Rage, we turn with our hostage and head back to see what's left of New Kirkham.

SIX

It's hard to tell what's going on from this far away, but the fact that thousands of zombies are milling around outside the walls makes it look like Jakob managed to shut the gate — otherwise they'd surely all have poured inside to feast. Whether he was in time to save the humans from the undead assailants who had already slipped in remains to be seen.

We quickly realise that getting Dan-Dan into New Kirkham is going to be a challenge. We can't just slip a living human through the hordes of zombies packed around the perimeter. All three of us would be ripped to pieces before we got anywhere near.

Rage comes up with a plan. 'I'll head back by myself. If anyone's still alive, I'll get them to tell us where the entrance to one of their tunnels is. We can sneak him in that way.'

'But the tunnel entrances are a secret,' I remind him. 'Vinyl wouldn't tell us before, said it was against the rules.'

Rage makes a growling noise. 'If Shane and the others have succeeded, we've just saved the town from the Ku Klux Klan. I think they'll be happy to bend the rules this once.'

He heads off, leaving me alone with the despicable Dan-Dan. I want the creep to cower, but he lies back, picks a blade of grass and studies the clouds, a content smile plastered across his face as he tickles his chin with the grass.

'Owl Man was wrong,' I say softly. 'I didn't like Vinyl that much. He'd moved to a different school. Our friendship had run its course. And the others mean nothing to me — we don't care about the living. You're dead meat.'

Dan-Dan chuckles. 'Nice try, but I've played poker with the finest gamblers in Las Vegas. Your bluff won't work on me.' He looks over. '*Owl Man*. I like it. That's what I'm going to call him from now on.'

'What's his real name?' I ask.

'Heaven knows. He changes it all the time. He's Petrus one day, Agamemnon the next, Zachary another. Occasionally Bob or Jack. Most of us refer to him as the guy with the large eyes, or simply Eyes Guy.' He pulls a face. 'Adults have such weak imaginations.'

I lie down close to Dan-Dan, hoping to make him feel uneasy. 'How did you hook up with Owl Man? Last I saw of you, you were zipping along the Thames like a bat out of hell.'

'Oh, we've been doing business together for years,' Dan-Dan says.

'Years?' I snap. 'You mean you knew him in the days before the zombies?'

'Yes. He knew the end was coming. He helped us prepare for it.'

'How did he know?' I bark.

Dan-Dan shrugs. 'He has his ways and means. Anyway, we've been allies for a long time. When the world fell, I made my base on HMS *Belfast* with the other members of the Board. Owl Man warned us against it. He said we'd be safer elsewhere, in a more secure facility. We ignored him, but had a plan B in place in case he was right. Hell, we had plans C, D and E.'

'And now?' I ask. 'Where have you holed up since we ran you off?'

He smiles. 'You'll find out when you swap me with your friend. I'm not going to tell you too much in advance, giving you extra time to scheme and plot against me. I'm not as dumb as I act.'

I glower at the giggling child-killer in the ridiculous sailor's outfit. I wish I didn't feel responsible for Vinyl and the others. I'd love to give this psycho a taste of his own medicine. But Owl Man read me like an X-ray. I'm not going to harm Dan-Dan as long as he holds the key to the humans' safety.

We don't say anything else. Dan-Dan watches the

sun as it moves across the sky and dips. I keep an eye out for Rage. Finally, not long before nightfall, he returns. He takes his time, not even bothering to jog.

'Glad you didn't rush on my account,' I growl when he crests the hill.

'Nothing to hurry back for,' he says. 'Everything's fine. Once we shook up the Klan and threw them into chaos, the tide swiftly turned. Biddy Barry and her crew got their hands on all the weapons that the Klan had come with, turned them on their owners and then on the zombies who'd poured through the gate while it was open. They lost a lot of people in the battle, but they've regained control of the town and their defences are solid. The surviving Klanners are being dealt with, as are the traitors who helped them take over the town in the first place. It's all cool.'

'And the tunnel?'

'Sorted. Follow me. One of the others is coming to open it from their end.'

The entrance isn't far away, a steel door set in the ground, covered over with very realistic-looking fake grass. Rage lifts the grass and knocks four times on the door. When it opens, I spot Shane inside. He scuttles out and high-fives his mate, knocks knuckles with me, then glares at Dan-Dan. 'This the one you were telling us about?'

'Yeah,' Rage says.

'The child-killer?'

'None other.'

Shane shows his fangs. 'Let's kill him.'

'Easy,' I intervene. 'We need this bugger alive so that we can swap him for all the people that the Klan took.'

Shane shakes his head. 'If we let him go, he'll kill more kids. I feel sorry for the prisoners who got carted off, but how can we justify letting this creep live when he'll probably go on to kill far more than the Klanners are holding hostage?'

'I didn't realise you thought about things so deeply.' I wasn't expecting an argument like this with the normally monosyllabic Shane.

'I might not be a genius,' Shane says, 'but I can count. If we return this merciless mug, we'll save sixty

or seventy lives — that's how many we think they got away with. But if we kill him, we'll maybe save hundreds.'

'Dan-Dan can't kill that many children,' I argue.

'Of course he can,' Rage says. 'He killed that many in the old days, if the rumours were true, and that was when the world was an orderly place. Now that he has a free hand, he could maybe run the numbers up into the thousands.'

'We agreed a deal,' I say stiffly.

'I didn't,' Shane replies and looks to Rage for support.

'I know where you're coming from,' Rage says after a pause to consider his answer, 'but I've got to side with B on this one. Lord Wood's a serious player. If we kill him, there will be repercussions.'

'Like what?' Shane snorts.

'Like blowing up your beloved County Hall for a start, you silly boy,' Dan-Dan snaps.

I'm surprised. 'I didn't think you knew about that.'

'We didn't,' he says. 'Not until your dashing Dr

Oystein rescued you and we were forced to flee the *Belfast*. Justin and I were furious. We were all set to send out a search party to track down the lot of you and exterminate you like the vermin that you are. Owl Man had to admit that he knew about you already. He didn't want your do-gooder of a doctor harmed. He wouldn't tell us his reasons, but he threatened to cut us off if we acted without his backing. We relented, since he is useful to us, but if you break our deal now, Justin will level the place.'

'Thanks for the warning,' Shane grins. 'We'll skip County Hall before she blows.' He raises a menacing hand and moves forward.

Rage and I block his path.

'That's not your call,' Rage says.

'County Hall is Dr Oystein's base,' I tell him. 'He's the only one who can make a decision like this.'

'We'll take the sap back with us,' Rage smiles. 'If Dr Oystein gives us the thumbs up, Dan-Dan's yours.'

'The hell he is,' I snarl. 'I want first dibs on him.'

Shane scowls. 'I don't care who kills him, just as long as he *is* killed.' He steps back. 'But you're right. It's for the doc to decide. Come on, let's hurry, I don't want to miss all the hangings.'

'*Hangings?*' I frown, but he's already jumped back into the tunnel. With an uneasy feeling, I let Rage and Dan-Dan go ahead of me, then follow after them, shutting the door on the world behind, before pressing through the gloom to face whatever storms are brewing in New Kirkham.

SEVEN

The town is awash with blood and corpses. The survivors are already gathering the bodies of the dead and cracking their skulls open for the brains inside — I guess they'll send most of them back with us, for the Angels to store and feast upon. It's a deal Dr Oystein has struck with many of the compounds.

When they've scraped the heads clean, they douse the bodies with petrol and add them to a growing mound which they'll set alight later. No time for any ceremonies. They can't leave the corpses rotting for fear they'd attract insects capable of spreading the zombie virus.

They've made a separate mound for the corpses of the undead, and Shane tells us that when the flames die down, a specially trained team will gather the remains and crush them up, then bag the bits and bury them deep. They have to be careful. Zombies are still contagious even after their brains have been destroyed.

The humans work in solemn silence. Some people are weeping, but only a few. Most have seen this before, when civilisation crashed. It's nothing new to them. There's work to be done. If they feel like crying, they'll save the tears for later.

Shane leads us to the main square, where the Ku Klux Klan were running riot just a few short hours ago. Now a lot of them are dangling from ropes. Biddy Barry and her crew have hanged them from lamp posts, chimneys, out of bedroom windows. Some are still alive, writhing while they choke, faces turning purple.

Others are being led to their death. Most don't go

quietly. They either beg for mercy or howl and curse their executioners. Quite a few laugh hysterically and vow to oversee the completion of their racist mission from Heaven.

The insiders who worked with the KKK are also being hanged. They're treated even more harshly, kicked and beaten as they're dragged along. Many are stripped and humiliated. Some are attacked and torn to death before they can be hoisted from the ground.

Biddy Barry is coordinating everything from the centre of the square. She roars commands at those around her, demanding updates, sending out scouts to sweep the town again, telling them to check under every bed and in every cupboard, not to overlook a single traitor or Klanner, to also make absolutely certain that no zombies remain at large.

The Angels are gathered nearby. I do a quick head-count and I'm pleased to see that everyone made it. Some are wounded, but all are standing, so I don't think any of the injuries are too serious.

'You should not have deserted us,' a grim-faced Ashtat criticises me as I join the group.

'I'd hardly call it deserting,' I protest. 'I had other fish to fry.' I nod at Dan-Dan, who's beaming at the hanging Klanners, approving of how they're being dealt with, showing his supposed allies not the slightest bit of loyalty.

'You should have helped us secure New Kirkham first,' Ashtat snaps. 'The hundreds of people here should have taken priority over the dozens on the trucks.'

I start to argue, but she's probably right, so I simply nod meekly.

'Any idea where they took the prisoners?' Carl asks.

'No. Fatty here will tell us later.'

'It's a good job I'm thick-skinned,' Dan-Dan sighs. 'You can be so hurtful.'

'Are you OK?' I ask Carl. His left arm is hanging loosely and there's a nasty gash along his forehead.

'Yeah. It happened in the crash. Nothing a dip in a Groove Tube can't cure.'

'And the rest of you?' I look around.

'I lost a couple of fingers,' Pearse says glumly, showing me his right hand.

I grimace. 'Did you save them? Dr Oystein might be able to reattach them.'

'That'd be hard,' he winces. 'A revived chewed them off and swallowed them. I didn't get a good look at its face. I'd have to slice open every corpse to try and find the fingers, and they probably wouldn't be in any shape to sew back on after an ordeal like that. I'm not bothered. I can do without them. As long as I'm able to scratch my bum, I'm happy. I won't even go in a Groove Tube, not for a minor thing like this.'

'That's stupid,' Conall huffs. 'Who are you trying to impress?'

'Not you, that's for sure,' Pearse retorts. 'Where were you when I was having my fingers bitten off?'

'Stopping the zombies behind that one from bashing your skull open,' Conall tells him. 'Now I wish I hadn't bothered.'

The pair scowl at one another, then laugh and knock knuckles, Pearse using his good left hand.

'Sorry I had to cut out on you,' I mumble to Jakob.

'You should be,' he says without looking at me. He's studying the hanging humans.

'But I did return with Dan-Dan,' I note. 'If we can swap him for the prisoners, my gamble was worth it, right?'

Jakob grunts. 'What about Owl Man? Did he get away with the others?'

'Yeah. I didn't get a chance to –'

I stop. I've just thought of something. I turn to Rage to ask him a question, but I'm interrupted by the booming tones of New Kirkham's mayor, the formidably blunt Biddy Barry.

'Is this the ruthless she-wolf who gave pursuit?' She steps up and beams at me. There are bloodstains on her Aran sweater and bruises on her cheeks where she was struck. But otherwise she looks much the same as she did when we first met earlier today. 'What's your name?'

'B Smith,' I answer.

'I admire the hell out of a girl who has the balls to think she can take down a couple of truckloads of fanatics by herself,' Biddy laughs. 'I'd shake your hand if I could, but the way things are, you'll under-stand why I'm keeping my distance.'

'No worries,' I smile.

'And you brought one back for us,' Biddy growls, eyeing Dan-Dan viciously.

'We need him to –'

'– swap for the captives,' she cuts me short. 'Yes, your hulk of a friend told us. I hate to lose any of my people, but are you sure they'd want us to let this worm off the hook? I read plenty of horror stories about Child Catcher Wood back in the day. If the choice was mine, he wouldn't be walking out of here in one piece, regardless of the dozens of lives that hang in the balance.'

'We can't think that way,' I disagree. 'We don't know how many children Dan-Dan will go on to murder. Maybe we'll get another chance to kill him before he can harm anyone else. Or he could have a heart attack.'

'He certainly looks ripe for a stroke,' Rage laughs.

'Hardly,' Dan-Dan retorts. 'I'm in perfect health. I'm just big-boned, is all.'

'We can't give up on them,' I tell the glowering mayor, ignoring Dan-Dan's contribution. 'If we don't fight for each and every survivor, we risk becoming like him.' I point at the child killer. 'Or them,' I add, nodding at some of the hanging Klanners.

Biddy Barry sighs. 'I don't like being given a lecture by a zombie, but I can see what you're saying. OK, Lord Wood is yours. But give him a little love bite from me once the others are in the clear, OK?'

'Tread carefully, Mayor Barry,' Dan-Dan says hotly, 'or I might decide to swing back through here one day and finish what I started.'

'If you ever swing back this way,' Biddy smiles sweetly, 'it won't be the only swinging you'll do.' She points at the dangling members of the Ku Klux Klan, then turns her back on us. 'Hate to love you and leave you, but I've got to make the hardest call of my life now.'

'What's that?' I ask.

She pauses to look back at me and her eyes fill with sadness. She jerks a thumb at a huge group of humans standing motionless at the far side of the square. I hadn't paid them any attention before. Now that I look more closely, I see they're being held in place by guards with guns.

'Those are the people who did nothing when the Klanners invaded,' she says, suddenly sounding weary. 'It's easy to deal with racist scum and traitors. But what do you do with people whose only real crime is cowardice?'

'You can't hang them!' I gasp.

Her features harden. 'That's what I have to figure out.'

As she marches away, I stare at the rest of the Angels with horror. 'Are we going to let this happen?'

'How can we stop it?' Carl asks glumly.

'There might be nothing to stop,' Ashtat says. 'They might settle it amicably.'

'And if they don't?' I bark.

Nobody says anything. They all look uneasy. Then Rage scratches the back of his head and scowls. 'Well, I guess we can either stay and watch the show, or head home early.'

'What the hell?' I yell.

'We're not human,' he snaps. 'We rescued these people from the Klanners and gave them back control of their town. Where they go from here is their business, not ours. We don't have any right to lay down the law for the living. We deal with our own and they deal with theirs. We wouldn't let them come to County Hall and call the shots, so we can't dictate to them here. It's their turf. Their people. Their *kind*.'

I stare at Rage miserably. 'But we can't just ... we have to ...'

'What?' Rage asks quietly. 'Fight Biddy Barry and her supporters? Kill them like we killed the Klanners? Take the side of the neutrals over those who tried to stop the Klan from doing whatever they wanted? That's our only option here, B. We're undead killing machines, not some diplomatic peace corps.'

I try to think of a response to that, but nothing comes to mind. I hate to admit it but he's right. We're powerless now that the fighting has stopped, just a bunch of living dead teenagers who can do nothing further to shape the destiny of the people we have saved.

'OK,' I croak. 'I'll keep out of it. Does that make you happy?'

'No,' Rage says glumly. 'This one time, I don't wish I was right at all.'

Then we trail after the mayor to watch events unfurl and find out if the living can be even more heartless and vengeful than the children of the damned.

EIGHT

It swiftly becomes apparent that the survivors who fought back are divided about those who stood by and let the KKK slice through the town at will.

About a hundred white people resisted. They're in control now, along with the three hundred or so black or foreign residents who were rescued and released.

Nobody made a case for the Klanners or traitors. Pretty much everyone agreed that they should be hanged. But it's harder for the group to decide what to do with those who took a neutral stance.

'Neutrality is no excuse,' an elderly man thunders.

'Those who stood by and did nothing are just as guilty as those who were rounding people up.'

'But they didn't do anything wrong,' a woman with two children argues. 'They were scared.'

'Some roared encouragement,' a black man growls. 'I saw a few of the bastards laughing and smiling.'

'Maybe,' the woman says. 'But many others were crying and shaking.'

'Should we split them up?' another woman asks. 'Save those who were afraid, hang those who were approving?'

'We can't punish a person just for smiling,' someone else protests.

The debate rages on. Biddy Barry listens silently, considering all arguments, letting everyone have their say. I do a rough headcount of the people being held. I reckon there's three hundred and fifty or thereabouts, mostly men and women, but some children too. Adding them to the four hundred or so judges, and those who were taken away on the trucks, I figure this town of a thousand people must have lost about two hundred souls to the Klanners or zombies.

As I'm counting, I spot Emma and Declan, the mother and son we escorted from London. They shouldn't be in there with the neutrals. They'd only just arrived, they didn't know anyone, the attack would have shocked them and left them with no idea who was on their side and who was against them. I want to call out to Emma, march across and drag her and Declan to safety, but when I catch Emma's eye, she looks away and wipes tears from her cheeks. It seems like she feels guilty, even if I don't think she should. And the other citizens of the town feel that way too. They're making no allowances.

Finally someone shouts for Biddy to give her opinion. Others take up the call and all faces turn in her direction. She nods softly and a hush falls over the crowd. Biddy looks around, measuring her words, then sighs.

'First things first. Does anyone want to punish the children?'

Nobody speaks up.

'OK,' Biddy yells to the people whose lives are on the line. 'Your kids can come to us. Whatever happens to the rest of you, they'll be safe. If you want to keep them with you, that's your right, we won't use force to take them. But in that case they'll be subject to the same judgement as the rest of you. Choose now.'

There's a round of hushed conversation. Lots of children start to cry. Many of their parents sob too. A few scream for justice and mercy, but are quickly shushed by their companions. Most of those under guard look as guilty as Emma and seem prepared to accept whatever comes their way.

Almost all of the children start moving across the square. Some are reluctant and are only stung into action when their parents roar or even hit them. They come weeping and trembling, gathering in a pitiful huddle, ignoring the attempts of the adults on our side of the divide to comfort them.

Some of the parents hold on to their kids, unable or unwilling to release them. I think they're selfish, yet I pity them. It must be horrible to abandon your young and face the threat of execution in front of their innocent eyes.

Declan is clinging to Emma. He's normally quiet as a mouse, but now he's shrieking, the sound of a siren's piercing wail, desperate to stay with his mother. Emma moans, prises his fingers loose and passes him to an older boy, who drags the kicking Declan out of the crowd of ghostly-looking adults. Emma turns away and wails. I feel wretched. If we hadn't brought them here, they would never have had to face this.

When all of the young have been sorted, Biddy addresses the crowd again. 'First we have to ask ourselves whether this settlement can continue with so great a loss. Can ... what ... four hundred-odd of us hold New Kirkham?'

'That won't be a problem,' someone huffs. 'It'll mean more space, food and water for the rest of us.'

'Supplies aren't an issue,' Biddy agrees. 'We can easily support a thousand, and more besides. But what happens if there's another attack like today's, if enemies like the Klan breach our defences again? We might need the extra support.'

'That lot weren't any help this time,' a woman

shouts. 'What makes you think they'd fight in the future?'

'Today caught us all off guard,' Biddy mutters. 'None of us expected an attack of this nature, to be turned on by our own people. We're alert to the threat now. I think they'd show more courage next time.'

'I do not care about *next time*,' an Indian man says. He's been holding a young boy in his arms. Now he raises the child and I realise the boy is dead. 'My son has been taken from me. Those people stood by and let it happen. They must pay.'

There are angry murmurings. The issue is discussed further, but the mood has swung. Most are in favour of retribution.

'OK,' Biddy says. 'If we're going to punish them, we have three options. We can construct a prison and keep them locked up for a period, maybe have them work for us while they're under lock and key, to pay their way. We can drive them into exile. Or we can hang them.'

People start muttering and arguing, but Biddy raises her voice to silence them. 'We could toss this back and forth for the rest of the night, and maybe that's what we'll end up doing, but let's have a show of hands first. Think hard for a minute, then vote. If we have a clear majority, we can save ourselves a lot of time.'

A hush falls again as people get their heads in order. Then Biddy calls for those in favour of imprisonment to show their support. Surprisingly, only twenty-six hands go up.

'Exile?' Biddy asks, and a forest of hands is instantly raised. 'Looks like we don't have to bother with the final option,' she says, and I can see she's relieved. I am too.

'It's not right,' someone bellows. 'They should be killed for what they did.'

'This is a democracy,' Biddy thunders. 'If you don't want to abide by the decision of the majority, you can join that lot by the wall.'

The challenger falls silent and there are no subsequent outcries.

'OK,' Biddy sniffs, calming down again. 'We'll keep them here tonight, then release them in the morning. Where they go after that is none of our business, as long as they don't try to come back.'

'You're sending us to our death,' a woman in the crowd of neutrals says. 'You might as well just execute us and have it over with.'

'That can easily be arranged,' Biddy says stiffly. 'Step forward if you'd rather face the noose.' Nobody moves. Biddy waits a moment, then smiles twistedly. 'I figured as much. Right, you can lie down and rest. We'll give you water and food in the morning, and make sure you can exit clear of any undead eyes. After that –'

'– they're dead meat,' Jakob cuts in, taking everyone by surprise.

'I don't think you lot have the right to get involved in this,' Biddy scowls.

'If we stand by and say nothing, aren't we as guilty as they've been?' Jakob retorts, nodding at the condemned. 'If their neutrality is a crime, surely we must be punished for it too?'

There's an uneasy silence. We're all staring at Jakob. Those of us who know him are more stunned than the others. He normally wouldn't say boo to a goose.

'Sending them into exile is the same as execution,' Jakob says, moving forward to stand close to the mayor, saying all the things I wanted to say, but couldn't get clear in my head. 'You're trying to kill them without staining your hands with their blood. They can't survive out there in that large a group. They'll attract attention and be killed.'

'Then let them split up,' Biddy says. 'They can leave in small groups, even individually. I'm not saying it will be easy, but some will make it to safety. Don't forget, we all had to find our way here in the first place.'

'If the zombie's that worried, let him guide them,' someone shouts, and lots of people laugh.

'I'll happily guide as many as I can if you drive them out,' Jakob says quietly. 'But who'll guide those of you who stay? When you lie awake at night, unable to sleep because of the torment you feel, who will offer you help? If you banish your friends, family and colleagues, you'll morally cut yourselves off from the world. How long can New Kirkham stand if everyone here hates themselves? How long do you *want* to stand in isolation and shame?'

'They're the ones who should be ashamed!' a woman screams.

'Yes,' Jakob says. 'And that shame is punishment enough. If you let them stay, and they have to work beside the rest of you every day, remembering that they let you down ...' He turns in a slow circle. 'How can they make right their wrongs if you don't give them a chance?'

There's a long silence. Then a black woman says, 'How could we trust them? How could we live with them, knowing they would have let us be taken?'

Jakob frowns and thinks about that. Then he grimaces. 'I have cancer. It was eating me away when I was alive. It stalled when I became a zombie, but it's still inside me. I can never cut it out. It's part of me. It hurts all the time. But I've learnt to adapt. I carry the pain around, I contain it, I control it.

'We all have weaknesses,' he continues. 'Life's a struggle for everyone. We can only overcome our flaws if we train ourselves to live with them.' Jakob steps back and lowers his head. 'That's all I have to say. My apologies if I've spoken out of turn.'

I'm half expecting a round of applause, but the silence holds. People are staring at Jakob and I doubt that most of them entirely know what to think.

Biddy Barry breaks the spell by shouting gruffly, 'Another show of hands. Who wants to keep them here and carry on as we were before?'

After a nervous pause, hands start going up, isolated at first, then a flood of them. It's not as big a majority as the pro-exile voters had a few minutes earlier, but it *is* a majority.

'Seems like we've had a change of heart,' Biddy chuckles. Her eyes narrow and she studies Jakob intently. 'But, as mayor of this lice-ridden hellhole of a town, I'm attaching a condition. If it isn't met, I'll push ahead with our original plan to exile the whole sorry lot of them.'

'What sort of a condition?' Jakob asks.

'I want you to stay and serve as my deputy mayor,' Biddy says, and if Jakob was capable of fainting with shock, he'd be out cold.

NINE

'What are you talking about?' Jakob splutters. He's not the only one who looks bewildered. The rest of us are also staring at Biddy Barry as if she's had a sudden mental breakdown.

'I want you to be my number two,' she says pleasantly, as if it's no big thing.

'You've got to be joking,' Jakob says. 'I don't live here.'

'You can move.'

'But I'm a zombie,' he reminds her.

'That's kind of obvious,' she snorts.

'You don't let zombies stay here. We're dangerous. We could infect one of you, maybe set off a chain reaction that would wipe out the town.'

Biddy shrugs. 'What's life without a hint of danger to spice things up?' As Jakob gawps at her, she faces the survivors of New Kirkham. 'I'm shocked and sickened by what happened today. I thought we'd put the old hatreds and fears behind us. I didn't think anyone could be worried about colour or religion at a time like this.

'I was wrong, and it's not often you'll hear me admitting that.' There are some rueful chuckles. 'We need to protect ourselves against those who would drag us back to the barbaric ways of the past. We're all equal here in New Kirkham – at least that's how I see it – and we have to make sure we keep sight of that.'

'How will taking in a zombie help us?' someone asks, glaring at Jakob.

'It will remind us that we can never afford to be prejudiced,' Biddy replies. 'I don't know about you, but I'm mortified that it took one of the undead to help us find mercy in ourselves. I assumed I was morally superior to every type of zombie, but how wrong was I?' She points at Jakob and the rest of us. 'When our lives were on the line, they risked all to help. They knew we mistrusted and disliked them, but that didn't deter them.

'I never thought of myself as being a racist,' Biddy sighs. 'But I see now that I was. I hated zombies, and that's no different to those creeps dangling above us. They hated blacks, Asians, Muslims. Ultimately it boils down to the same thing — hatred of those who aren't the same as us.'

'It's not the same thing at all,' an Asian woman growls. 'I've had to deal with hatemongers all my life. But I *do* deal with them. You can work around a racist, turn a blind eye to their insults, strike out if they push things too far. You can't do that with a zombie. If a racist hits me, I can hit back. But one scratch from that guy and I'm damned.'

'So we'll tread carefully around him,' Biddy says. 'It'll be good for us. It will drive home the fact that we need to be on our guard all the time, that we can't sail through life without paying attention to those around us.

'I can't force this on you,' Biddy tells the crowd. 'This is a democracy. If you're not with me, you can vote me out. But if you want me to stay on as mayor, you'll have to accept ... hell, I don't even know his name.' She raises an eyebrow at Jakob.

'Jakob Pegg,' he says weakly.

'If you want me, Jakob's part of the package,' Biddy declares. 'I've always governed as I see fit, regardless of whether my policies are popular or not. That's paid off so far, so I'm hoping you'll trust me on this one too. We need this guy to keep us on the straight and narrow, to remind us why we put up with the suffering and fighting and fear, to help keep the bigots and racists at bay.

'Show of hands again,' Biddy booms. 'You're either for me or against me. If it's the latter, I'll step aside without a word of complaint and leave New Kirkham, because it won't be the sort of place where I want to live. If we're going to restart society, we might as well try to do it the right way.

'If you want me to stay, and if you're prepared to accept Jakob Pegg as my deputy, stick your hand in the air to show that you care.'

Nobody responds for a few seconds. They stare at Biddy, then at each other, not sure what to make of her startling ultimatum. Then a couple of hands go up. A few more. Then a wave of them, at least three-quarters of the people assembled, not just those who fought the KKK, but the neutrals too.

'That's what I like to see,' Biddy chuckles. 'People with their heads screwed on. So, zombie boy, it looks like you don't have a choice.'

'I could refuse,' Jakob says quietly. 'Just leave with the others and return to London.'

'You could,' Biddy nods. 'But if I'm any judge, based on that speech you gave, you won't.'

Jakob licks his lips – old habits die hard – then looks to the rest of us to see what we think.

'No point running this by us,' Carl smiles. 'This is way over our heads.'

'What will Dr Oystein think if I don't return?' Jakob asks.

'He'll be glad to be rid of your cancer-ridden carcass,' Rage snorts.

'Ignore the lunk,' I growl, elbowing Rage in the ribs. 'The doc won't mind. He'll understand when we tell him how it happened.'

'I think he will be proud of you,' Ashtat says. 'I know that I certainly am.'

'But don't feel under any pressure,' I add. 'You don't owe them. If you don't want to do this, feel free to turn them down.'

'You don't think the doc will see this as a dereliction of duty?' Jakob asks. 'There are so many battles to be fought . . .'

'Yeah,' Shane grunts, 'but he's always said that we're fighting for people like this. If we get the better of Mr Dowling, we'll hand power back to the living and let them rule the world again. I think the doc will be chuffed if you help these guys hang on in there, so that they can take over from us once we're done kicking arse.'

'That was almost poetical,' I murmur.

'Thanks,' Shane grins.

'*Almost.*'

He shoots me the finger and laughs.

Jakob thinks about it some more. 'I'll miss you guys if I stay,' he whispers.

'We will miss you too,' Ashtat says, and the rest of us mutter similar things, except for Rage, who rolls his eyes and makes a gagging gesture.

'We'll see you when we bring newcomers,' Pearse says.

'We'll keep you up to date,' Conall promises. 'Tell you everything that's going on back in County Hall.'

'And you can always leave if you get sick of it here,' Carl notes. 'You're not signing up for life.' He chuckles. 'You're dead, so you can't.'

Jakob nods slowly, then faces Biddy Barry again. 'In that case there's a condition of my own that you'll have to meet.'

'Fire away,' Biddy scowls, not sure what to expect.

With a straight face, Jakob says, 'I'll only do it if I get a badge. I was a big fan of Westerns when I was alive, and I've always wanted a deputy sheriff's star.'

TEN

We retire to a quiet corner of the square for the night, leaving Jakob and the humans to deal with the dead and start the job of getting their town back in order. The neutrals who have been spared exile slot sheepishly into place, parents like Emma gratefully reuniting with their children before wiping their tears away and buckling down to try to make good.

Shortly before eleven, Dan-Dan yawns. 'I never was much of a night bird,' he says. 'And we have a big day ahead of us. So I'll wish you all sweet dreams.'

He blows us a kiss, rolls over and is asleep within minutes.

'That guy's unbelievable,' Shane laughs. 'You've got to admire his guts. It's like he doesn't care that we're zombies.'

'He'd care if he woke up to find us tickling him,' I snarl.

We pass the time resting and chatting. I feel agitated after the battle for New Kirkham, but I calm down as the hours slip by. I keep reminding myself that we did a good thing today, saved many lives, wrestled control of the town back from the Ku Klux Klan. It doesn't feel like a real victory because I failed to rescue Vinyl and the others who were being held in the trucks that got away, but this is definitely one for our side. Hundreds of people are free tonight because we fought for what was right.

Jakob comes to see us shortly before dawn. He still looks dazed.

'Should we bow, Your Worship?' Rage smirks.

'If you like,' Jakob says with a thin smile, then sinks down next to us and shakes his head. 'I can't believe I let her talk me into this. It's madness. They'll never accept me as one of their own. I should sneak out with you guys.'

'Dr Oystein would not like that,' Ashtat says. 'This is the first time that one of us has made a bridge of this sort. It could be the start of a new relationship between us and them. If things work out, maybe other communities will see the benefit of having an Angel on their team. This could help draw the living and the undead closer together.'

'Or it could backfire and drive us even further apart,' Rage chortles. 'I'm glad I'm not in your shoes.'

'As supportive and sympathetic as always,' Jakob murmurs, then smiles at the rest of us. 'I meant what I said earlier. I'll miss you. You've been my family since I found my way to County Hall. Things won't be the same without you.'

'Are you going to be OK by yourself?' Pearse asks.

'One of us can stay with you if you want,' Conall says.

'Thanks, but I'll be fine,' Jakob says. 'They were going to send the brains from the corpses back with you guys, but you need to move swiftly, and such a load would slow you down, so they're going to freeze and store most of them here for the time being, meaning I won't go hungry.'

'Maybe you will fatten up now,' Ashtat grins. Jakob doesn't have to reply. He knows she's joking. None of us can ever bulk up or slim down. Those days are long behind us.

'Is there anything you want us to bring the next time we come?' Pearse asks.

'No,' Jakob says. 'Nothing there really mattered to me. Except you lot.'

'Pass me the sick bucket,' Rage groans, but we ignore him.

We spend a pleasant hour talking with Jakob, the world growing lighter around us, then get ready to depart. Before we set off, we have an unexpected visitor. Shy Declan comes creeping forward. He's holding something behind his back.

'Hi, little guy,' I mutter, smiling awkwardly when he stops in front of me. I look for his mother and spot her lurking in the shadows of a house across the square. I wave to her, but she draws further back into the shade. I figure she's too ashamed to face us in person, even though I don't think that she should be.

Declan produces his surprise. It's my Australian hat. I cast it aside before we went into battle yesterday.

'How did you find that?' I yelp with delight. I start to reach for it, then remember that I have to be careful. 'Can you place it on the ground, please?'

Declan does as I ask, then takes a step back, giving me room to safely pick up the hat. I settle it on my head and grin at the others. 'How do I look?'

'Like the world's dumbest explorer,' Rage huffs.

'Bite me,' I laugh. 'I love this hat. I've had it since before I came to County Hall. Thank you, Declan. This means a lot to me.'

Declan nods, beaming, and turns to rejoin his mother. Then he looks back at us. His eyes are solemn as he gulps and says in a soft, creaky voice, 'Thanks.'

As I stare at him with a lump in my throat, he

smiles quickly, then races over to where Emma is waiting.

'A cute kid,' Pearse says.

'Yeah,' I whisper. Then, scowling at myself for being a sap, I slip back into my normal mode and shout at the sleeping creep behind us. 'Hey! Child Catcher! Wakey-wakey!'

Dan-Dan rolls towards us and opens an eye. 'Morning already? Time slips by so fast.' He stands, stretches, then undoes his flies and pees in open view of us all.

'Gross!' Carl gags.

'That's not something I need to see this early in the day,' Carl mutters.

'You are disgusting,' Ashtat snarls, turning her back on him.

'Ah,' Rage says nostalgically. 'That brings back happy memories. I miss my first whizz of the day.'

'What?' Dan-Dan smirks as he tucks himself away. 'It's not like anyone who matters is present. I don't care what I do in front of a pack of walking corpses.'

'Come on,' Pearse says. 'We've a long way to go, a

lot of ground to cover. Let's not waste any more time. Unless you plan to follow that up with a poo?'

Dan-Dan blinks. 'Hardly. Some acts are never to be shared, even with the undead.' Then he catches sight of someone passing and shouts out, 'Mayor Barry! A moment of your time, please.'

Biddy Barry stops and waits for Dan-Dan to waddle over to her. 'What do you want, worm?'

'We found ourselves in a heated situation yesterday,' Dan-Dan simpers. 'Harsh words were exchanged. I wanted to have a quick discussion now that everyone has calmed down.'

'I'm not in a discussing mood,' Biddy rumbles. 'If you've something to say, spit it out quick.'

'Very well,' Dan-Dan says cheerfully. 'You know who I am.'

'A child-killing creep,' Biddy grunts.

'An incredibly powerful, influential child-killing creep,' Dan-Dan corrects her with a smug chuckle. 'I've no heartfelt interest in the Ku Klux Klan. I was using them because they could deliver the children I required. It doesn't bother me in the slightest that you've hanged so many of them. In fact, I admire the no-nonsense way you people went about your work.'

'Thanks,' Biddy says with mock sweetness. 'That means so much to me.'

'What I'm trying to say,' Dan-Dan murmurs, 'is we don't have to be enemies. We could do business together.'

'What sort of business?' Biddy frowns.

'For a start, I could return your people, the ones who were taken.'

'They'll be sent back to us anyway when the Angels deliver you to your allies,' Biddy notes.

'Maybe, maybe not,' Dan-Dan replies. 'Owl Man said he would try to arrange for their release, but he was in no position to make such a guarantee. I, on the other hand, *am* in that position. If you agree a deal with me, I'll have them sent back in perfect health, along with any supplies that you might be in the market for.'

Biddy's eyes narrow. 'That's a generous offer, Lord Wood. What would we have to do for you in return?'

'Grant me safe passage home,' Dan-Dan says, then

nods at us. 'And serve me up their heads on several nicely sharpened sticks. That's all I ask. Everything else will be forgotten and forgiven.'

Biddy chews her lower lip, thinking it over. Then she looks past Dan-Dan. 'Deputy Pegg? What's your take on this?'

'I think we should ram his offer up his arse,' Jakob roars.

'Your position has been duly noted.' Biddy faces Dan-Dan again. 'Get stuffed, scumbag,' she says, and walks away briskly.

'Now there's a woman with style,' Dan-Dan chortles, not in the least offended. 'I knew it was a long shot, but nothing ventured, nothing gained. Shall we head off then, my little undead retinue, or is there time for brekkie before we set sail?'

'Eat this, fat boy,' I growl, giving him the finger. Then we bid Jakob a final farewell, wish him luck, crawl down into a tunnel that has been sanctioned for our use, and set off on the long trek home.

ELEVEN

We push the pace heading back to London, mindful of the deadline. We should have plenty of time to return to County Hall, then head over to wherever Owl Man is and swap the child-killer for the prisoners, but there's always a risk we might get delayed along the way.

I expect the chubby Lord to struggle to keep up with us, but to my surprise he's very sprightly, marching along, whistling softly and trying to make small talk.

'Keep it quiet, fatso,' I growl at him at one point. 'You'll draw zombies down on us.'

'I trust you to defend me if that happens,' Dan-Dan smiles, then carries on whistling the same as before. He clearly thinks he has a charmed life.

The sickening thing is that the creep *does* seem to have been blessed with good luck. We're targeted by a trickle of zombies over the course of the day, but we never come under serious threat. They're always in small groups and easy to deal with. Dan-Dan even whips out his smartphone a few times to take pictures. He might not be able to get a signal these days, but the camera still functions.

'Smile for me, B,' he sings as I wrestle with a zombie twice my size.

I almost set the zombie loose and sic it on the would-be sailor. Then I think of Vinyl and the other humans and hold tight.

Dan-Dan spends a lot of the time slyly trying to bribe us. He offers us riches and privileges, luxury villas on zombie-free islands, all the fresh brains we could ask for. We ignore him, except for Rage, who pretends to be interested. At least I hope he's just pretending!

We hit the suburbs of London late in the evening. If we were by ourselves, we'd push on, but the zombies will be emerging in their multitudes soon. Suburbia is dangerous for one of the living at the best of times – the attacks have picked up sharply over the last hour – and it would be suicide to parade around with Dan-Dan once the sun has set.

Pearse and Conall scout out a few houses until they find one that's free of zombies and relatively easy to defend. It also offers an escape option via the roof, though if we have to flee with Dan-Dan in the dark, when the streets are awash with zombies, escape will probably only offer him a temporary respite. Even lucky buggers like him have their limits.

Dan-Dan knows this is serious. He quits whistling, settles down in a room with no windows and munches quietly on an energy bar — he has a stash of them stored in various pockets.

'Not so lively now, are you?' I murmur wickedly as he eats.

Dan-Dan shrugs. 'I'm not a fool,' he whispers. 'I know when to turn the volume down.'

113

Once the house has been secured, Rage sniffs and says, 'I'm off.'

'Where are you going?' Shane asks.

'To see a man about a horse,' Rage deadpans.

'This doesn't have anything to do with Dan-Dan's offers, does it?' I growl, worried that Rage might be heading out to bring back help for the child-killer.

'Give me *some* credit,' Rage snaps. 'I'm a cynical sod, and proud of it, but I'm not *that* cynical. Cut a deal with the murderous likes of Daniel Wood? Hardly.'

'So where are you going?' I press.

'There's something I'm curious about. A little mystery I want to solve. I would have dealt with it before this if we hadn't been sent off on a mission. Now that I've got some free time on my hands, this seems as good an opportunity as any.'

'But we are still *on* the mission,' Ashtat notes. 'We will need you if zombies attack.'

'Nah,' Rage laughs. 'I won't make much of a difference if that happens. Besides, I'm kind of hoping they *do* attack. You should all slope off if they do, leave Dan-Dan on his own, see how smug he is then.'

'I really think you should stay,' Carl says stiffly.

'Tough,' Rage sniffs. 'Don't worry, I'll be back before you leave in the morning, ready to pitch in and help when needed. If you want to rat me out to Dr Oystein when we get home, feel free.'

And with that he's off.

The rest of us stare at one another, troubled, but since there's nothing we can do about it, we close the door after him and return to the room where Dan-Dan has holed up, to serve as his reluctant guards for the night.

Dan-Dan spends the next few hours dangling more bribes in front of us. I don't think he expects us to accept, and we could tell him to shut up, but we're amused by what he comes up with and the way he tries to sell himself. Dan-Dan is smooth as silk. I have to keep reminding myself that he's a vile piece of filth, in order to stop myself starting to like the guy.

Finally, shortly after ten, Dan-Dan yawns and calls

it a night. 'Think about what we've been discussing,' he purrs. 'If you change your minds, let me know in the morning and we can thrash out a deal.'

'Don't you want us to wake you with the news?' I smile.

'Heavens, no,' Dan-Dan says. 'A good night's sleep is sacrosanct. I've had people shot for disturbing my slumber.'

He settles down and is snoring lightly moments later.

'I hate him,' Ashtat says softly, 'but I can see why he got away with his crimes for so long. As well as being rich, he could charm even the gruffest of people.'

'Yeah,' I nod. 'I bet he's sweet-talked his way out of all sorts of jams in his time.'

'The islands sound nice,' Shane reflects.

'You're not seriously considering his offers?' I hiss.

'Of course not,' he growls. 'I'm just saying I like the sound of the islands. Maybe we could check them out ourselves when this is over.'

'Yeah,' Carl says. 'There'll be all the time in the

world for sightseeing once we're done with Mr Dowling. I'd love to visit the Seychelles again. It's been too long.'

'I prefer Skegness,' Shane says and we all laugh, but quietly, so as not to alert any passing monsters outside.

Rage returns about an hour before dawn. He's got a face like a slapped arse and his hands are trembling.

'What's up?' I ask as he lets himself into the room and slumps in a corner, looking like a gambler who lost everything at the races.

'Shut it,' he says.

'Did you try to woo a zombie?' I simper. 'Did she turn you down?'

Rage stares at me as if he's thinking of killing me. I don't wilt. I know from experience that you can never show fear in front of a bully.

'What's wrong?' Shane asks quietly, concerned about his friend.

'Nothing,' Rage snaps. Then he forces a weak smile. 'I just found out tonight that I was right never to believe in the goodness of man. We're all a bunch of skunks when you strip away the trimmings, every stinking last one of us. I've always known the world was peppered with bastards like Dan-Dan, but I thought they were balanced out by decent, well-meaning people. I was a fool. We're all as worthless as that snoring killer, every single one of us.'

'You're in a cheerful mood,' Carl snorts.

'Yeah, well,' Rage drawls, leaning back against the wall to stare at the ceiling. And he doesn't say anything else after that.

We rise an hour later, as the sun is starting to come up. Dan-Dan slips off to the bathroom to do his business – 'Time for a number two,' he cheerfully informs us – and comes out with his nose pinched shut. 'Quick,' he croaks. 'Let's get the hell out of here. If that stench doesn't attract the undead hordes, I don't know what will.'

We head off in high spirits, except for the glowering Rage, as if the slaughter we'd witnessed in New Kirkham was months ago instead of just hours behind us. It's nice to be closing in on home. We haven't been away very long, but it feels like weeks.

I'm looking forward to catching up with the others, resting in my own bed, tucking into Ciara's cranial stew. Of course there's still Vinyl and his fellow captives to worry about, but I put thoughts of them to one side for the time being and focus on all the joys of County Hall.

Attacks come more regularly than yesterday and we're kept busy saving Dan-Dan's rotten neck. He's not as chirpy today. Marching through the middle of London is a different proposition to tramping through the countryside. Zombies can attack at any moment, from the shadows of any building. We're on constant alert, no room for error.

Despite the frequency of the assaults, our luck holds and we advance without casualty through the suburbs, then the parks of central London. After a swift dash through Westminster Square, we catch sight of the stunning County Hall building. Excited, we jog across Westminster Bridge and are soon being welcomed back by our fellow Angels. They're delighted to see us, curious about Dan-Dan, anxious when they note Jakob's absence. We assure them that

everything's fine, promise to fill them in on all the details later, then ask if Dr Oystein is around. They tell us he's in his laboratory and we make a beeline for it.

The doc spots us through the glass of the lab door and hurries out into the courtyard to greet us. He's smiling warmly, arms spread wide. Then he spots Dan-Dan and draws to a halt. Nobody says anything for a moment while we wait for Dr Oystein to compose himself.

'It is good to see you again, my Angels,' he murmurs. 'But I must admit I am surprised by the company you are keeping.'

'This is –' I begin to tell him.

'– Lord Daniel Wood,' Dr Oystein cuts in. 'I recognise him from pictures I've seen in the past, but even without them I would have known him from your accurate description after your stay on the *Belfast*. I see that his penchant for naval outfits remains.'

'You can't go wrong with a good sailor's costume,' Dan-Dan smirks, then adds, 'I know you too. I've heard many tales about the fabulous Dr Oystein. Our owl-eyed friend is full of them.'

'You consort with him now?' Dr Oystein asks coldly.

'Oh yes. We're the best of friends.'

The doc mulls that over, then looks around and frowns. 'Jakob is not with you. Is he . . .?'

'Don't worry, he's fine,' I tell him.

'He's become the deputy mayor of New Kirkham,' Shane says and the doc stares at us uncertainly. 'Honestly. I'm not kidding.'

'It sounds as if you have had a most unusual adventure,' the doc mutters.

'And it's not over yet,' I growl. 'The KKK took Vinyl and a load of other people prisoner. Owl Man wants us to swap Dan-Dan for them. That's why we haven't ripped his throat out.'

'Yet,' Shane adds for good measure.

Dr Oystein looks astonished. 'This is grave, unsettling news. You must tell me the full story. Zhang will need to hear it too. Give me a few minutes to finish up. I will meet all of you in Zhang's rooms presently.'

As we turn to leave, the doctor calls to Dan-Dan. 'Lord Wood, I welcome you to County Hall and offer you my protection during your stay with us.'

'Very kind of you,' Dan-Dan says, taken aback.

'But if you even look sideways at any of my young Angels,' the doc says softly but firmly, 'I will tear your flesh from your bones in as slow and excruciating a manner as possible. And bear in mind that I have had decades to consider such procedures.'

As Dan-Dan's cheeks redden in a rare moment of unconcealed terror, Dr Oystein says, 'Get this piece of rotting flotsam out of my sight,' then heads back into his lab to tidy up and cool down.

I've never seen the doc that worked up before. I have to say, it was a delicious surprise. If I could bottle Dan-Dan's expression, I'd take pleasure from it every single day for the rest of my life. Take *that*, you putrid, child-killing scum!

TWELVE

We find Master Zhang training a group of Angels. We interrupt and tell him that Dr Oystein is coming. He dismisses his students and bids us sit. While we're waiting, he fetches a kettle, teapots and cups, then starts to brew tea. He loved flavoured tea when he was alive, and even though we can't taste much now, he likes to indulge his old habit.

Zhang hands a cup to each of us, inviting us to test his concoction. He pauses when he comes to Dan-Dan, then sets down a cup in front of him and bows politely, as he has done with the rest of us.

'Many thanks,' Dan-Dan says, returning the bow. Then he says something in Chinese. Zhang looks startled, but responds in his own tongue. The pair exchange a few sentences – I think it's part of the traditional ceremony – then Dan-Dan bows again, picks up the cup and sips. 'Delicious,' he sighs happily. 'This brings back many sweet memories.'

'I suppose China was one of your stomping grounds in the bad old days,' I sneer.

'As I told you, I was a global traveller,' Dan-Dan beams, sipping the tea again. 'But I must admit, I spent more time in the Far East than elsewhere. I found their lack of hypocrisy refreshing.'

'You're saying we're hypocrites because we despise you?' Carl snorts.

'No,' Dan-Dan says. 'You upstanding young ladies and gentlemen have ignored my bribes and promises of rewards if you set me free. I respect you for that. I can understand your reasons for not wanting to do business with a rogue like me. There were many people who shared your view and had nothing to do with me in the past. I never had a problem with that.

If you'll pardon the pun, I know I'm not everyone's cup of tea.

'But there were others who were willing to overlook what I got up to in my spare time. You'd be shocked by the number of politicians, police officers, judges, lawyers and journalists who were happy to take my money and look the other way when I was plucking my darlings from the streets and slitting their tender throats. Now, if they'd left it at that, I wouldn't have a bad word said about them. But many were two-faced. They gladly accepted my bribes, but spoke ill of me behind my back and in public, as if they were better than me.

'That wasn't the case with my Far Eastern contacts. If they chose to deal with me, they accepted that they were as culpable as I was. If you do business with a depraved beast – as many regard me, although of course I don't share their warped view – you automatically lower yourself to that level. My Eastern friends didn't have the airs and graces of their Western counterparts. I tell you, children, I'm guilty of many sins, but I think hypocrisy is the worst of all, and of that I am innocent.'

We start to argue with him, but before we get very far, Dr Oystein appears and silence falls. He accepts a cup of tea from Master Zhang, but doesn't drink any of it. He's staring at Dan-Dan, looking angrier but at the same time more troubled than I've ever seen him.

'Tell me what happened,' he finally says, and we fill him in on all the twists of our mission, connecting with Vinyl and the survivors in Hammersmith, making it to New Kirkham, spotting Owl Man and the Ku Klux Klan on our way back. We tell him how we returned to the town and fought. I describe my pursuit of the trucks and my run-in with Owl Man. I expect him to comment on that, but he says nothing. We finish with Jakob staying on at Biddy Barry's invitation to serve as her deputy.

'Extraordinary,' Dr Oystein murmurs, his first word since he asked for our story. 'Jakob will be a fine ambassador. This could be the beginning of a vital new phase for us.'

'That is what I said,' Ashtat beams.

'But as for everything else . . .' Dr Oystein's face

clouds over again. He shares a questioning glance with Master Zhang. Our mentor hesitates, then nods.

'Come with me, please, Lord Wood,' Zhang says, getting to his feet.

'Where are you taking me?' Dan-Dan asks as he rises, looking ever so slightly worried.

'A room where you can rest and dine,' Zhang says. 'Our chef, Ciara, will take your order and serve you as best she can.'

'What about exchanging me for the girl's friend and the other prisoners?' Dan-Dan asks Dr Oystein. 'You're not going to renege on our deal, are you?'

'I agreed no deal with you,' Dr Oystein says quietly.

Dan-Dan stiffens. 'My allies will kill the lot of them most brutally if you don't take me back.'

'I am aware of that,' Dr Oystein replies. Then, having given Dan-Dan a few seconds to sweat, he looks at me and smiles briefly. 'Allay your fears, Lord Wood. We will return you to Battersea Power Station safe and sound, as promised.'

Dan-Dan gawps. 'You know where I'm based?'

Dr Oystein nods. 'I have eyes everywhere. I know

where Owl Man and the members of the Klan have situated themselves, so if you are working together as closely as you intimated, I assume that is where you have also set up home.'

'Then why haven't you ...?' Dan-Dan frowns, then shrugs. 'No, it's none of my business. I'm peckish. I'll go see what your people can rustle up for me. Just one question first. When will I be leaving?'

'Either this afternoon or tomorrow morning,' Dr Oystein says.

'Excellent,' Dan-Dan grins and waddles off after Master Zhang.

'What a horrible excuse for a man,' Dr Oystein says sourly. 'It is not often that I can find nothing good to say about someone, but Lord Wood is vile through and through.'

'He does things with style though,' Rage chuckles, smiling for the first time since he returned to us after his mysterious night on the town.

'Admittedly,' Dr Oystein says. 'He is a powerful, dangerous adversary. Many did not take him seriously in the past, because of his buffoonish appearance. All of those walked away the worse for their encounters. I will not underestimate him.'

The doc falls silent. We wait for him to speak, but although my patience has improved vastly since I started training here, I can't contain myself indefinitely, and I'm the one who finally breaks the thoughtful peace. 'You knew about the Ku Klux Klan?'

'Yes,' Dr Oystein says.

'Why didn't you tell us?'

He sighs. 'I was hoping the army would deal with them. As worrying as they are, Mr Dowling must be our priority, and I was afraid that some of you might get distracted if you knew about those marauding monsters. I did not consider them our problem.'

'Well, they're our problem now,' I snort. 'We have to free the prisoners, make Owl Man release them as he promised, in return for Dan-Dan.'

Dr Oystein frowns. 'But you said he only guaranteed your friend's release.'

'Yeah, but he said he'd do his best to have the others freed too.'

'And you think that he will honour his pledge?' Dr Oystein asks.

'Yes,' I say confidently. 'I didn't when we were discussing it, and only went along with him because I had no choice. But I've been thinking about it since then, and I've realised he didn't have to strike the deal in the first place, so I'm more optimistic that he'll do what he said he would, that it's a deal he made because he wanted to make it, not because we were forcing his hand.'

Dr Oystein looks confused. 'What do you mean?'

'Owl Man didn't work his voodoo on Rage.' I turn to face the bewildered hulk. 'You didn't feel anything strange when you were holding Dan-Dan, did you, like you should release him and step away?'

'No,' Rage squints. 'Why should I?'

'When I tried to attack Owl Man's dog in New Kirkham, he took control of my body.' I describe what happened, how I lost the ability to move, how he turned me into a puppet, manipulating me with his words alone. 'If he could do that to me, he can probably do it to other revitaliseds,' I conclude. 'So why didn't he do it to Rage and simply take Dan-Dan there and then?'

'Maybe I'm stronger willed than you,' Rage smirks.

'I doubt it,' I sniff. 'He can control reviveds, the same way the mutants can, and I think he must be able to do that with revitaliseds too.'

'No,' Dr Oystein says. 'Reviveds obey orders instinctively. They are placid among themselves – they never fight with one another – and they will follow the leadership of any undead creature who directs them. We could train ourselves to command them in that fashion, except I think it would be an abuse of our power.

'This is different. It must be something he set up in the past. You told me that you had crossed paths with Owl Man before the zombie rising, that he knew some of your most intimate secrets.'

'Yeah,' I mutter, remembering the day he visited my flat, how my dad was afraid of him, how he knew about my nightmares.

'I still do not know why he is interested in you,' Dr Oystein says, 'but he was obviously keeping an eye on you before you were turned. He must have hypnotised you at some point.'

'Seriously?' I gawp.

'It is not as difficult as it sounds. He could have done it through third parties, your teachers for instance, instructed them to use key words or phrases in a deliberate way, at specific times, so that you would respond to certain commands later.'

'I don't think any of my teachers were that bright,' I say dubiously.

'Then it might have been a doctor, a nurse, anyone. It is a worrying Achilles' heel, but it is a personal defect. He was not able to pull that trick on Rage because he had not established control over him prior to their meeting.'

'Whatever,' I shrug. 'I still think he'll let the others go in exchange for Dan-Dan. I don't know what sort of a thing they have going, but he nearly shat a brick when Dan-Dan threatened to withdraw his support.'

'What if he refuses to sanction the swap?' Carl asks.

'Then we use force,' I growl. 'We hit them hard, free the prisoners, give those hooded horrors hell.'

'Amen to that!' Carl cries sarcastically.

'You don't want to do anything about it?' I shout at him.

'Of course I do,' he says. 'I just don't think it's as easy as you're making out. We don't know how many of them there are, or what sort of weaponry they might be packing. We can't just storm in, knock them about and trot back home victoriously.'

'You did it when you rescued me from HMS *Belfast*,' I remind him.

'That was different. Barnes gave us the inside scoop, told us how many guards were onboard, helped us distract them. We knew what we were getting into. This time we don't.'

'But we know they're in Battersea Power Station,' Shane says. 'That's a massive place. They can't have covered every angle, no matter how careful they've been. If they won't release all the prisoners, we can scout it out, find a weak spot, then hit them when they least expect it.'

'No,' Dr Oystein says before I can respond. 'We . . .' He pauses. Master Zhang is returning. The doc waits until he's comfortably seated again, then continues. 'We cannot take any action against these people at the moment.'

'Why not?' I thunder. 'You raided the *Belfast* to help me. Are you saying the people of New Kirkham aren't as important as I was?'

'This is more complicated,' he sighs. 'We are now dealing with an element that we must be wary of. We cannot wade in as we could anywhere else.'

'Why the hell not?' I shout, losing my temper.

Dr Oystein runs a hand through his thin, brown, greying hair. 'To answer that question,' he says glumly, 'I will have to share secrets with you which I have so far withheld from my Angels.' He checks with Master Zhang again – our mentor gives no indication of what he might be thinking – then makes up his mind. 'Yes, it is time.'

'Time for what?' I groan, hating the intrigue. But the doc stuns me into silence with his next softly delivered line.

'It is time,' he whispers, 'to tell you about Owl Man and the terrible link that we share.'

THIRTEEN

'His real name, if it matters, is Tom White,' Dr Oystein says. 'For some reason he never liked that. He felt it was too ordinary. He used to make up exotic-sounding names for himself. His favourite was Zachary.'

'He calls his dog Sakarias, which is similar,' I note.

'He has a dog?' Dr Oystein asks, and I tell him about the mutant sheepdog. 'How strange. He experimented on animals in the past, but I thought he had moved on from that. Perhaps he simply felt the need for a pet. God knows, he is a lonely soul.

'Anyway, Tom White was recommended to me by a contact in Cambridge. I was told he was an extraordinary young scientist with similar interests to my own. An interview was arranged. Apart from the oddity of him insisting I refer to him as Zachary, we got along splendidly. He was bright, warm, amusing. He was clearly a genius, so I would have invited him to join my team regardless of his personality, but I also felt that we could become friends . . .'

They became very close friends in the end. Dr Oystein describes their work together, the tests they conducted, the breakthroughs they made in their quest to counteract the zombie gene. *Zachary* became Dr Oystein's most trusted and valuable assistant. He helped the doctor develop the vaccine which allowed me and the other Angels to revitalise.

'I had been working on it for a long time without making much progress,' Dr Oystein says. 'With Zachary's help, I made huge strides within a few years.'

Zachary was never happy with the finished, unstable vaccine. He kept trying to refine it, to rid it of its destructive elements, so that it could be given to every living human.

'Of course I was disturbed by its instability as well,' Dr Oystein says. 'But I was more of a realist than Zachary.' He pauses. 'Or perhaps I was simply more inhuman.'

Zachary wanted to wait until they had perfected the vaccine before they tested it on living subjects. Dr Oystein ignored his assistant's wishes and pushed ahead with the programme. He had no idea when the zombie virus would break out and sweep the globe. He only knew that time was against them and he was determined to fight back with whatever tools they had at their disposal, every step of the way.

The pair of friends argued fiercely about it. Dr Oystein knew that thousands of lives would be wasted, and to him that was an acceptable loss. He would grieve for every person that was sacrificed, but he was prepared to accept the grief and the guilt.

'It weighed heavier on Zachary's mind,' the doc sighs. 'He went along with my instructions reluctantly, but in retrospect I think he should have

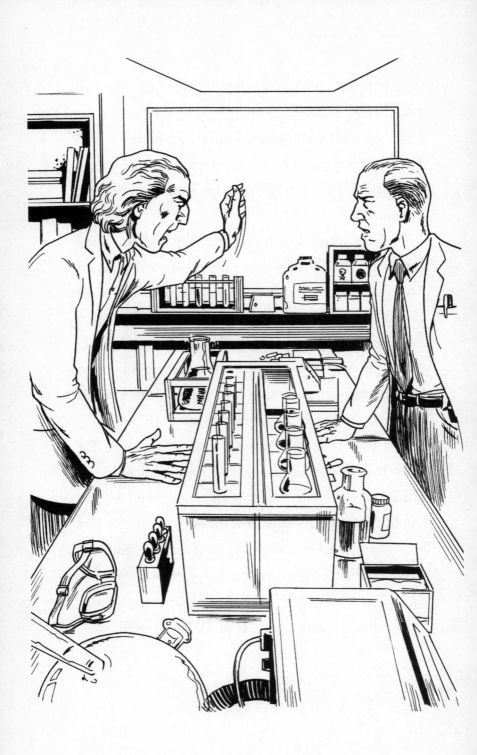

stepped aside. It hit him hard and changed him. I was too caught up in our studies to notice. By the time I realised that something had radically altered in him, it was too late.'

The vaccine wasn't their sole hope of defeating the zombie hordes. It was their Holy Grail – if they had been able to fine-tune it, they could have vaccinated the entire population and stopped the zombie apocalypse before it could start – but not their only weapon. So, while they pressed on with refining the vaccine, they also focused on how they would cope if the era of the living dead came to pass.

They worked hard on a virus which would attack the brains of the undead, one that could spread as swiftly as the zombie gene would. A virus designed to drop every reanimated corpse in its tracks. It would be the ultimate in chemical warfare, a way of wiping out their enemies in one fell swoop.

'It's a pity you didn't get anywhere with that,' Carl says. 'We could end this here and now if you had.'

'It would kill us too,' Shane notes.

Carl shrugs. 'We've all got to go sometime.'

Dr Oystein says nothing. He shares another troubled look with Master Zhang, who nods slightly and says, 'They succeeded. The virus exists.'

There's a shocked silence. We stare at Master Zhang, then at Dr Oystein.

'I do not understand,' Ashtat frowns.

'You're saying you have a virus that can kill every zombie?' I bark.

'Yes,' Dr Oystein says. 'I call it Clements-13, after the woman my brother was married to, and her year of birth.' He smiles. 'Strange that I cannot remember my own birthday, but I have never forgotten hers or my wife's.

'Clements-13 is a dark red liquid. It is so potent that one vial is all we would need to release. Within a couple of weeks, it would have cloned itself endlessly and spread to every last corner of the world, penetrating even the most otherwise impenetrable of bunkers. The war would be over. The living would be victorious. Every zombie would be dead.'

'Then what the hell are we doing sitting here talking about it?' I roar, leaping to my feet. 'Get me the damn vial. I'll smash it open and end this thing today.'

'We cannot do that,' Dr Oystein whispers.

'Why?' I shout. 'Because we'd die too? I don't care. If it means saving what's left of mankind, I'll take the fall. Let them stick up a statue in our honour, or forget about us entirely. What does it matter?'

'Whoa,' Shane says. 'Let's not be hasty here.'

'Can it, you coward,' I snap, then hold out my hand to Dr Oystein, clicking my fingers as if summoning a dog.

'Show respect or I will admonish you,' Zhang growls.

'You can shut up too,' I retort. 'I can't believe the pair of you have let us go through all this ... let the survivors suffer for all these months ... when you can stop the madness by breaking open one little vial.'

'You do us proud, B,' Dr Oystein smiles. 'I am delighted that you are willing to sacrifice yourself for the lives of others.'

'I wouldn't have been a year or two ago,' I huff. 'But life hasn't been a barrel of laughs since I revitalised.' I frown and slowly sit down again. 'But you told us you didn't care about yourself either. You said you'd happily pass the reins of power back to the living if you got the better of Mr Dowling, that it would be a relief to roll over and die for real.'

'Yes.' Dr Oystein looks down at his hands and his voice drops. 'To be honest, I long for the end. To pass from this realm, to know the blessedness of eternal sleep, to be embraced by our maker ... it is what I yearn for more than anything else.'

'Then what's stopping you from unleashing Clements-13?' I ask quietly, but part of me has already figured out the answer.

'There is another virus,' the doc croaks. 'It can wipe out the living as swiftly as Clements-13 can destroy the undead. But the keeper of that vial is neither human nor zombie. My nemesis ... our most feared foe ... *Mr Dowling* has it.'

FOURTEEN

There's a long, horrified silence. Then Dr Oystein continues.

'I do not claim to understand the state of Zachary's mind. I got to know him well before our paths diverged, and I have studied him at length from afar since. But I cannot say with certainty what he wants from this life or why he acts as he does. I have only my theories . . .'

In his last few years as the doctor's assistant, Zachary mentioned Dr Oystein's longevity a couple of times. He spoke of all the good that he could do with those centuries at his disposal, the different fields he could branch out into. He said it was a shame that Dr Oystein would be killed by the virus if they were successful in cultivating it. He suggested they work on a form of the virus that might spare revitaliseds while annihilating reviveds.

Dr Oystein had no interest in surviving the zombie apocalypse. In his view the world could only be truly safe if it was rid of every last member of the undead. Zachary nodded solemnly when that was put to him, admitted the doc was right and seemed to leave the matter there.

'Science always demands a price,' Dr Oystein says, wearily massaging his forehead. 'Before we could develop a virus that might work on the undead, we had to find one that would work on the living. It was the only way we could move forward.'

The doc immersed himself in his research, developing deadly viruses in controlled environments, experimenting on live subjects supplied to him by the armies and political parties that he was in league with.

'We struck a Faustian pact,' he mutters. 'I needed the human guinea pigs and technical resources which they could supply. In return I offered them the promise of chemical weapons and, even more tempting than that, prolonged life.'

Dr Oystein knew from an early stage that the zombie gene could exist in a variety of states. He had created the reviveds and was working on revitaliseds. But there were mutant strains too, weird permutations of the gene which gave birth to creatures caught between the worlds of the living and the dead.

'I had no interest in the more twisted strains,' he says. 'But there was a man who was obsessed by them — Mr Dowling.'

The doc doesn't know much about Mr Dowling's background, how he became aware of the work which had been initiated by the Nazis. But, as mad as he was in other ways, his scientific genius rivalled that of Dr Oystein. He was as brilliant in his laboratory as he was insane outside of it, working in opposition to the doc and his assistants, concocting his own wild versions of the undead gene.

'He toyed with his subjects,' Dr Oystein tells us. 'The mutants and the inhuman baby that B saw were the results of his tinkering. There might be others that we are not aware of.'

Dr Oystein developed a virus which would swiftly purge the earth of its human inhabitants if released. It was a nasty but ingenious little number. It would leave all the other creatures unharmed, only wiping out humanity and maybe some genetically close simians, like chimpanzees and gorillas. The virus in its purest form was a milky white liquid. It had a long chemical description, but the doc christened it Schlesinger-10, after his wife and her year of birth.

He kept Schlesinger-10 under lock and key. Only four other people had access to it. He trusted each of them implicitly. They were family as far as he was concerned. Zachary was one of the four.

The doc thinks that Zachary became fixated on cheating death. He might have been nobly motivated to begin with – live longer in order to help mankind – but things got warped inside his head somewhere along the way.

The virus was a threat to his plans. When Dr Oystein produced Schlesinger-10, Zachary knew it was only a matter of time before it was adapted to work on zombies. When that happened, the doctor would safely dispose of his samples of Schlesinger-10, then unleash the zombie-destroying virus when the war between the living and the undead began.

'Putting the pieces together after the fact,' the doc goes on, 'I realised that Zachary must have initiated contact with Mr Dowling around that time. Or perhaps Mr Dowling approached him. Either way, they struck a deal and Mr Dowling injected Zachary with a unique mutant strain. It allows Zachary to live normally to most intents and purposes, with a heartbeat and functioning internal organs, yet to age slowly. From what I have seen, he does not age as slowly as us, so I do not think he will live as long, but he has extended his lifespan by several centuries at least.'

'Is the injection why his eyes are so large?' I ask.

Dr Oystein nods. 'They were big before, but nowhere near as owl-like as they are now. The pot belly was another side effect. I have no idea why he should have ballooned out in that fashion. I think it took Zachary by surprise too. He was always rather proud of his slim physique.'

Once Zachary had been injected – or perhaps the injection came later, the doc isn't sure – he set about stealing Schlesinger-10 and killing all of those who could replicate it. It was a swift, vicious coup. He sneaked Mr Dowling's mutants into the laboratory where Schlesinger-10 was stored. Other mutants targeted Dr Oystein and the three colleagues of his who had worked directly on the virus.

'The mutants killed my assistants,' the doc moans, the horror of the loss still reflected in his expression all these years later. 'I should have been executed too. They caught me by surprise. Zachary had granted them access to my living quarters, where I was normally alone.'

'So what happened?' I ask when the doc doesn't continue. 'Did you find your inner warrior and give them the licking of a lifetime?'

'Tea,' Master Zhang answers quietly. 'He was saved by my fondness for tea.'

The doc felt weary that night. Zhang spotted him on his way to his room. He looked as if he was about to keel over with exhaustion. Zhang offered to make tea for him. He thought the process of brewing and sipping tea would help him relax.

Dr Oystein almost never invited anyone back to his room, which was what Zachary had been relying on. But the doc appreciated the offer of company that night, and let Zhang come with his pot and cups.

'I was more than the doctor's assailants had bargained for,' Zhang says. 'They came prepared for a man of peace. I was an unexpected added ingredient.'

Zhang fought like a tiger – the doc's description – and disabled the six mutants who had been assigned the task of killing Zachary's primary target. The pair raced to the lab and sounded the alarm, but their foes had already struck and retreated. And Zachary had taken the vial of Schlesinger-10 with him, along with all of the notes relating to it.

'The paperwork was nothing,' Dr Oystein sniffs. 'I was able to reproduce the virus within weeks. But he gave the sample which he had taken to Mr Dowling, and that changed everything.'

'Why didn't the clown use it straight away, before you developed the zombie-killing version?' I frown.

'I'm not sure,' the doc says. 'Perhaps he wanted to conduct more experiments on the living before he disposed of them. Once the virus is released, there can be no going back. Anybody would be wary of opening such a Pandora's box, even one as mentally unhinged as Mr Dowling.'

'But he *will* open it if we force his hand by directly attacking him or Zachary,' Zhang says. 'That is why we cannot target Battersea Power Station.'

'Zachary and Mr Dowling are thick as thieves,' Dr Oystein says, 'so we have had to deal with my ex-assistant very carefully since he betrayed us. If we struck at his base, Mr Dowling might retaliate by opening his vial of Schlesinger-10.'

'He wouldn't dare,' I mutter. 'Even if you didn't release your virus, zombies can't reproduce. They'd all die off within a couple of thousand years. He'd be the king of a doomed kingdom.'

'You are forgetting about the babies,' Dr Oystein murmurs, and I feel a chill race up and down my spine. 'The babies in your dreams, and the one you saw in real life. We think they have been developed to provide Mr Dowling with fresh subjects in the centuries to come. They are mutant clones and, if we are right, Mr Dowling is setting them up to become the populace of the future.

'The only thing stopping Mr Dowling from wiping out mankind is that he knows I would retaliate with Clements-13, which I perfected a few years after Zachary betrayed me. As things stand, we are deadlocked. If one of us releases his virus, the other will retaliate by releasing theirs, and that will mean the end for us all. Neither of us wishes to see that happen, but if we stood poised to kill Zachary or Mr Dowling, he would almost certainly unleash the hellish harpies of Schlesinger-10 which are his to command, so that our victory would be a short-lived affair.

'We cannot risk it, B,' he finishes softly. 'That is why, if their captors refuse to release the prisoners, we can do no more than swap Dan-Dan for your friend. The others – not just those from New Kirkham, but the hundreds or thousands who have been taken from other towns – are beyond our help. Our hands are tied. I wish with all my heart that it was not so, but . . .'

The doc shrugs miserably, a simple gesture of defeat and dismay, and I know in that moment that unless I can convince Owl Man to set free the others – and the more I think about it, the less chance there seems to be that he will – then all of those poor souls are damned.

FIFTEEN

We're a glum lot when the doc finishes. Nobody says anything for ages. Rage is the only one who doesn't look desolate. He's smiling away to himself, as if this is all one big joke.

'Does this mean our hands will always be tied?' Carl finally asks. 'I thought we were going to tackle Mr Dowling one day. Are you saying we can never do that?'

Dr Oystein sighs. '*Never* is a very long time. I do not know where Mr Dowling stores his vial of Schlesinger-10. Perhaps he carries it around with him, or maybe he keeps it somewhere safe. If we find out, we can devise a plan of action and either launch a raid or set out to incapacitate Mr Dowling. Or maybe one of his mutants or Zachary will turn on him and kill him for us.'

'In that case, wouldn't his killer take the vial if Mr Dowling keeps it with him?' I ask.

'Or, if it is held elsewhere, would Mr Dowling not have instructed some of his people to retrieve the virus if he is killed?' Ashtat chips in.

Dr Oystein grimaces. 'All those outcomes and many more are possible. That is why we must bide our time and hope for the best.' He rises and groans, rubbing his most recent wound, where he was shot by my ex-teacher Billy Burke. 'I know this is unsettling news. That is why I hold certain information back, so as not to disturb the rest of you. But, when times call for it, I must reluctantly share the burden. My apologies for troubling you with this.'

'It's not your fault, doc,' Carl says. 'Don't beat yourself up over it.'

The doc smiles gratefully at Carl, then strokes his

chin thoughtfully. 'Now we must deal with the more pressing matter of what to do with Lord Wood. Are you sure you want to return him, B? You know how cruel he is. Do you really wish to set him free to torment and kill again?'

'No,' I mutter. 'But Vinyl's my mate, and there's still a chance that Owl Man might arrange the release of the others too. I can't just abandon them. Of course, if you insist on keeping Dan-Dan . . .'

'I am sorry,' he says. 'I will not force you to obey me. I was not the one who risked all in pursuit of the trucks or who took Daniel captive. He is your prisoner, not mine. You have earned the right to do with him as you see fit.'

'Actually, *I* was the one who captured him,' Rage sniffs. 'But I'm happy to leave this to Becky. I don't care what happens to the sadistic sod.'

I wrestle with the dilemma for a minute, then my shoulders slump. 'Even if I can't get the rest of them released, I've got to do it for Vinyl. If we hand Dan-Dan back to them, we can target him another time, hopefully before he can do any more harm. But if we execute him now, Owl Man will definitely kill Vinyl. I couldn't live with that on my conscience.'

'I understand,' Dr Oystein says, offering me a comforting smile. 'Then we will return Daniel this afternoon. I know we have until tomorrow, but I would rather not leave it until the last moment. Now, who will I send to escort him?' He looks around.

'I'll go,' I volunteer. 'I kind of have to, don't I?'

To my surprise, Dr Oystein responds with a firm, 'No. You are the one person we cannot send.'

'What are you talking about?' I snap.

'Owl Man, you idiot,' Rage growls. 'He can control you, so he could turn you against the rest of us.'

'He didn't before,' I pout.

'Because I had Dan-Dan in my grip,' Rage reminds me. 'He couldn't turn you on me because Dan-Dan might have been nicked by one of us.'

'I dunno,' I mumble. 'He never worked that trick on me any of the other times we've met. It was only when I pointed the gun at his dog.'

'Even so,' Dr Oystein says, 'we cannot risk it. You must stay with us. We will all be safer that way.'

He studies his Angels again. 'Rage?'

Rage looks uncertain for a second. A worried look crosses his face. He starts to say something. Then he changes his mind and grins. 'Count me in, doc. I was the one who hooked the slimy fish, so I guess it's only fitting that I take him the rest of the way.'

'And . . .' Dr Oystein's gaze settles on Pearse and Conall, but then he notices Pearse's missing fingers. 'You are injured.'

'It's nothing major,' Pearse says, although I can tell by his wince that the pain is greater than he's admitting.

'You need to spend some time in a Groove Tube,' the doc says.

'Maybe later. Not now. I'm good to go if you want me.'

'Are you sure?' Dr Oystein presses.

Pearse nods. 'I won't let you down.'

Dr Oystein hesitates. He stares again at the other Angels. Then he nods. 'Very well. I had another assignment in mind for the pair of you, but I suppose you can deal with it once you have delivered your package. Go see Ciara. Eat heartily. Then have Zhang examine your wound, to be sure it is not more serious than you think. After that, come to me in my laboratory.

'Rage, will you accompany me now? We can discuss the best way to handle the swap, to ensure you cannot be double-crossed. Zachary is usually trustworthy in situations like this, but it pays to be cautious.'

'No probs, doc,' Rage says. 'I believe in covering all angles.'

'The rest of you can return to your room and rest,' Dr Oystein says. 'You have done well and I am proud of you.'

As the others are filing out, Dr Oystein calls me back. He clasps my arms and stares into my eyes. 'I know this has not been an easy decision. But you have made it and you must live with it. Do not be harsh on yourself. As you noted, we will hopefully get another chance to bring Lord Wood to justice later.'

I nod glumly, then look questioningly at the ancient scientist. 'Am I doing the right thing? Should I have sacrificed Vinyl for the greater good?'

The doc cocks his head. 'There is no sure answer to that. In your position I would not have let Daniel leave, even if the other prisoners were a confirmed part of the equation. More lives will be lost once we return him. But, as I said earlier, sacrifices are inevitable in this ghastly, grisly war. We cannot save everyone, so we are forced to choose who to spare and who to let perish.

'I deliberately vaccinated hundreds of thousands of children, aware that the vast majority would die horribly, in order to produce a team of Angels. I cannot provide you with a moral compass,' he says hollowly, 'because I lost my own many decades ago. We do what we think is right. After that, we can only pray that we choose the correct path, and hope our maker will forgive us if we err.

'If it is any consolation,' he adds in a whisper, 'I have done far worse than you ever will.' Then he squeezes my shoulders – the only comfort he can offer – and leaves me to brood over whether or not a damned wretch like me has the right to bother the Almighty with her prayers.

SIXTEEN

In the end I don't pray, but I do a hell of a lot of brooding. At first I wander the corridors of County Hall, trying to get my head straight, to reassure myself that I'm making the right choice. But I keep bumping into Angels who want to know how our mission went. The distractions annoy me.

There are loads of places in County Hall where I could go to get away from everyone, but for some reason I'm drawn to one in particular. I have to ask a couple of Angels to find out where he is, and then it takes me a while to locate it, but eventually I'm sitting in a small room with no windows, a bed, a tray of dried-out scraps of brain and my old teacher, Billy Burke.

Mr Dowling got his hands on Burke and messed with his mind. The clown sent him to kill Dr Oystein. To protect the doc, I had to disarm my ex-teacher. I wounded him during the process and he was infected. Chalk up another one for team zombie.

Burke asked to be vaccinated when he was human. Very few adults respond to the vaccination, but he liked to think there would be some sliver of hope that he could be restored if he was turned. I wanted to kill him when he became a zombie – I hate the thought of him shuffling around in this drooling state – but felt I owed him the chance that he'd requested. So we kept him alive and imprisoned him, so that he wouldn't run after Ciara or Reilly or any of the other humans who occasionally stay with us.

Burke doesn't recognise me when I unlock the door and slip into his cell. He must have fed recently, because he's smiling softly, standing by the bed, rubbing his stomach. He barely even zones in long enough to check that I'm not a member of the living. Then his gaze goes distant again.

The bed sheets are ruffled, but I doubt he lies down too often. Zombies have to shelter from the sun every day, but usually they squat or lean against a wall when they're at rest. Some lie down out of dimly-remembered habit, but most have forgotten that beds are for relaxing. I wouldn't have bothered putting one in the cell, but Dr Oystein likes to treat everyone with dignity.

'I bet neither of us thought it would end like this back when we were teacher and student,' I murmur, staring sadly at the blank-faced empty vessel of a man. 'What a mess.'

I think again about what Dr Oystein told us. As if Mr Dowling, mutants and zombies weren't enough, now we've got to add Schlesinger-10 to our list of obstacles to overcome. And maybe there are even grimmer secrets that the doc hasn't told us about yet. I can appreciate that he wants to break the bad news to us gradually, but I'd rather have it all out in the open. I don't think anything is scarier than the threats you aren't aware of.

'I wish I could discuss this with you,' I tell the disinterested zombie. 'You were always straight up with me. You helped me see things clearly when I wasn't sure of them myself.'

I frown and think back to some of our conversations. Burke warned me not to follow my racist, bullying dad's example, not to let my angry father do as he liked without challenging him. In class he would encourage us to listen to ourselves before anyone else, not to automatically trust politicians, teachers or our parents. If we saw an injustice, we should act on it, regardless of what anyone else told us.

'You wouldn't have let Dan-Dan go,' I mutter. 'But I can't believe you'd have given up on Vinyl and the rest of the prisoners either. Is there something else I can offer Owl Man? Maybe trade myself for them?'

Owl Man is interested in me for some dark, twisted reason, but he was prepared to let Dan-Dan kill me in order to keep the powerful Child Catcher onside. I can't see why he would have changed his mind about that overnight. Dan-Dan seems to be more valuable to him than I am.

Offer him Dr Oystein's head on a plate? I dismiss the idea before it fully forms. I'm sure Owl Man would jump at that, but I wouldn't give up the doc for anything.

No matter what way I look at it, I can't see an alternative. So I come at the problem from a different angle. Is there a way to make the swap and then kill Dan-Dan?

My eyes narrow. I'm not sure how they'll arrange the trade. That's what Dr Oystein is discussing with Rage. But I'm guessing they'll have to do it in a way that guarantees the safety of both Vinyl – and the others if they can persuade Owl Man to add them to the deal – and Dan-Dan. In movies, where spies are swapped, they're sometimes released to walk past one another, with snipers on both sides keeping the pair in sight the whole way — if one of them is harmed, the others can retaliate instantly.

That won't work in this case, since only Dan-Dan's mob will have guns. Maybe one of the Angels will advance with Dan-Dan, finger to his throat, acting as a virtual rifle. It would be risky. I can't see why they'd let the revitalised walk away once he releases Dan-Dan — they could simply shoot him. Maybe have someone else return with the Angel, someone valuable to them, just not as valuable as Dan-Dan, for that person to be released once the Angel's in the clear?

Whatever way they go about it, I definitely think an Angel will have to stick by Dan-Dan's side until the swap has been completed. If it was me, I could wait until Vinyl was safe, then slit Dan-Dan's throat. It would mean my execution, but at least I'd have rescued my friend and put an end to Dan-Dan's butchering ways.

How would Owl Man react? He wouldn't be happy, but he'd surely know it was a personal decision, nothing to do with Dr Oystein. He wouldn't strike back if I'd been killed in return. An eye for an eye, a zombie for a child-killer. Hell, if Owl Man was close, overseeing the swap, maybe I could throw myself at him, twist that long neck of his before his aides could stop me, kill two birds with one undead stone. *That* would be a good day's work!

I chuckle at the thought of taking both of the monsters down. Then I consider the plan seriously. It's unlikely that I'd be able to get to Owl Man. And it's possible he'd use his hold over me to stop me killing Dan-Dan. But if he didn't think there was a threat ... if he wasn't expecting me to sacrifice myself ...

I'm sure Dr Oystein wouldn't approve. The world's full of vicious killers. We'll never be able to get rid of them all. The subtraction of a single piece of scum won't make much of a difference one way or the other. Revitaliseds on the other hand are a very limited commodity. In his eyes I'm far more important than a creep like Daniel Wood. He wouldn't see the child-killer as being worth the price of one of his Angels.

But I haven't had a high opinion of myself since I came back to life. Dr Oystein sees more in me than

I ever will. And I'm the one who would have to live with the guilt every time Dan-Dan killed. Every life he claimed would be traceable back to my decision to set him free. Dr Oystein can cope with that sort of burden. I can't.

'He's going to be mad at me,' I tell Mr Burke. 'He might not understand why I did it. But you would have. You might have tried to talk me out of it. Maybe you'd have found a way of making things even out. But, with no better plan on the table, and the choice a simple one between letting Dan-Dan carry on killing or putting a stop to his wicked ways . . .

'You always told us to listen to our hearts, and mine is telling me to ignore the doc, take matters into my own hands and end this today. Well, I don't have an actual heart, but you know what I mean, don't you?'

The zombie doesn't respond, but I pretend that Billy Burke has given me the thumbs up. 'Thanks, boss,' I grin as I let myself out. 'That's what I needed to hear.'

And that marks the end of B Smith toeing the party line. I'm back to going it alone, trusting my instincts, dealing with the world in my own crude fashion. It's probably not the wisest move I've ever made. And it will almost certainly be my last. But you know what? I don't care. Because at least I'm taking my destiny in my hands and deciding my future. Besides, if this is such a wrong move, why do I feel so damned *good* about it?

Watch out, Dan-Dan, here I come!

SEVENTEEN

I'd like to go to my room, change out of my filthy clothes, bid farewell to Ashtat and the others — they've been good friends and I hate the thought of just cutting out on them. But they'd ask questions. They'd want to know where I was going. If they guessed what I was planning, they might rat me out to Dr Oystein, not to spite me, but because they wouldn't want to see me throw away my future like this. They're a solid crew. I'll miss them.

I have my wide-brimmed hat and a replacement pair of prescription sunglasses for those I lost in New

Kirkham and, although my clothes are on the tattered side, they'll protect me from the sun. A quick visit to the kitchen where Ciara stores the brains, a munch to ensure I'm at my physical peak, then I'm good to go.

I slip out of County Hall and head west along the Albert Embankment. It's quiet, not a single zombie on the prowl. The Thames is calm, no bodies floating past today. A lone pigeon flaps by overhead. A rare survivor. It must be one of the more cunning of its kind. Most have had their heads ripped off by zombies.

I consider where to plant myself. I have to hook up with Rage and his team before they get to the power station. I don't dare do it too close to Battersea, as I'm sure the others will argue with me and it's best not to have a slanging match in front of a load of gun-toting Klanners. But equally I don't want to give Rage too much time to think about it. His first reaction will be to turn back and report me to the doc. He'll be less likely to do that if he has to make a trek.

Battersea Power Station isn't that far from County

Hall, an easy three-quarters-of-an-hour hike. I'm surprised none of us swung by before and noticed all the hooded figures that had made themselves at home. Although now that I consider it, our official scouting orders always directed us away from that area. Dr Oystein and Master Zhang weren't obvious about it. They just never sent us anywhere near.

I'm sure some of the Angels have passed by regardless and clocked the activity within. But they would have told the doc or Zhang, who probably asked them to keep it quiet, so as not to disturb the rest of us. In fairness to the cautious pair, I wouldn't have felt so at ease all these months knowing that our enemies were camped nearby.

I decide to wait by the gleaming glass buildings of Vauxhall, more than halfway along a road called Nine Elms Lane. I choose an open area and settle down.

I have to endure a longer wait than anticipated. An hour passes slowly. Another. Still no sign of them. The sun is starting to sink. I worry that they've decided to wait until morning or, even worse, that they took a different route. I can't imagine why they would have. This is the most direct approach. But maybe Dr Oystein told them to go a roundabout way.

As I'm on the verge of deserting my post to check what's happening at the power station, I spot them skulking towards me. I'd know it was them even if I wasn't expecting them — there's no mistaking skinny Pearse in his beekeeper's hat, face hidden behind the mesh. And Conall and Rage have to be the biggest pair of teenage behemoths stalking the streets of London.

Dan-Dan is between Pearse and Conall, Rage just behind the trio. All of the Angels are alert, checking the doorways and windows of every building, pausing any time a shadow flickers. Dan-Dan is silent. He doesn't look nervous, but definitely more sombre than he was on our way back from New Kirkham.

Conall clocks me while they're still a good distance away. He holds up a hand and they stop. I stand, take off my hat and slowly wave it over my head. They

can't see my face, but they can tell from my gesture that I'm no ordinary revived. They have a quick confab, then Conall comes trotting towards me. He stops when he realises who it is.

'What are you doing here?' he asks.

'Working on my tan,' I joke.

'You're not supposed to be here. Dr Oystein told you to stay in County Hall.'

'Looks like I disobeyed him,' I sniff. 'You gonna court-martial me?' Conall stares at me, bewildered. 'Just call over the others. We can sort it out between us.'

Rage is furious when Conall fetches him. I've never seen him so angry, and he's someone who rarely passes for placid at the best of times.

'I'm gonna kick your arse all the way back to County Hall,' he snarls.

'You'll have to,' I tell him, 'because I won't go quietly.'

'What the hell are you playing at? Weren't you listening to the doc? You're a threat. Owl Man can turn you against us.'

'I don't think he will.'

'*Think?*' Rage explodes. 'If you were capable of rational thought, you'd have stayed where you were told. Get out of here, Smith, before I go to town on you.'

'You and whose army?' I challenge him.

'I'm serious,' he says coldly, stepping forward, fingers clenching. 'I'll beat you to within an inch of your worthless, irritating excuse for a life.'

'Bring it on, big boy,' I retort without budging, never one to back down when put on the spot, even when faced with a foe who's packing way more muscle than me.

'Children, children,' Dan-Dan murmurs behind us.

'Stay out of this, fat man,' I snap, giving Rage the evil eye while I wait for him to take a swing at me.

'Believe me, I would like nothing better than to watch the pair of you duke it out,' Dan-Dan giggles. 'It would be a scintillating scrap, and I'm not at all sure who I'd bet on if I was to gamble. But you will draw unwanted attention. If you kick up a fuss, the undead will investigate. Not a problem for those of you who lack a heartbeat, but it would be a serious inconvenience for yours truly.'

'We can deal with a few reviveds,' Rage snorts.

'Not if they come in their hundreds,' Dan-Dan says.

'He's right, 'Pearse mutters. 'You can't do this here. It's too open.'

'That's what she banked on,' Conall says with disgust.

'I always was a clever girl,' I snicker, then focus on Rage. 'I'm coming.'

'No.'

'I need to do this. Vinyl was my best friend, and I think we'll have a better chance of convincing Owl Man to let the others go if I'm on the scene.'

'I don't care.'

'I won't go back.'

'Then I'll tie you up and leave you here.'

'Not without me making the mother of all rackets.'

'You wouldn't,' he says, but I can tell by his

expression that he's not sure. My presence has thrown him. He wasn't expecting this.

'I won't interfere,' I promise, lying through my teeth. 'But I can't sit by and do nothing. If something goes wrong – if they try to trick you, or if you're attacked on your way back – I'd spend the rest of my days wondering if I could have made a difference.'

'B,' Rage says softly, a rare use of my favoured name, 'don't put me in this position. Dr Oystein tasked me with ensuring this goes smoothly. Let me do my job. You can wait here for us if you want, help escort Vinyl back from this point. And I'll do everything I can to have the other humans released too. How does that sound?'

'Like a fair compromise,' I nod.

Rage starts to smile. Then he catches my smirk and curses. 'You never were one for compromise, were you?' he says gruffly.

'Not when I was alive. Definitely not since I died.'

'You're going to regret it if you come,' he warns me.

183

'Maybe. It won't be the first time I've ignored sound advice and gone on to rue the day.'

Rage hesitates, weighing up his options.

'We can return to County Hall,' Conall suggests. 'Tell Dr Oystein. Leave it to him to sort her out.'

'Then you won't be able to bring Dan-Dan back today,' I note. 'And I'll still be waiting in this spot tomorrow.'

'Maybe we won't swap him at all,' Pearse jeers. 'Vinyl's your best friend, not ours. If you're going to be a stubborn fool, maybe we'll just let them kill him and take care of Dan-Dan ourselves.'

Dan-Dan blanches. 'Easy, young fellow. Let's not do something hasty that we'll all regret later.'

'Last chance, B,' Rage says. 'Wise up and keep out of this.'

I shrug helplessly. 'I can't.'

'OK,' he says. 'If you're that damn keen to tag along, on your own head be it. I'll lead. Fall in behind and cover the rest of us. You might as well make yourself useful.'

'Anything you say, boss.'

Rage shoots me a dirty look and moves forward. I slip to the rear of the group, relieved and surprised that it wasn't more difficult than that. Pearse and Conall take up their positions either side of Dan-Dan. Rage looks back, makes sure we're all where we should be. Then he jerks his head, points a finger and we advance.

EIGHTEEN

As we're turning off Nine Elms Lane, Rage pauses and looks back. 'Change places with me.'

'Why?' I ask suspiciously.

'I want you to push ahead, so if there are any traps, you'll trigger them first.'

'How considerate of you,' I snap.

'Hey,' he says, 'I don't want you here. If you'd rather back out, be my guest. Otherwise take the crap job and be thankful we're letting you be part of this at all.'

I give Rage the finger, but slip ahead of the group

as ordered. I edge along, ready to throw myself aside if I get the slightest scent of a trap.

I negotiate the road without any problems and come to the area surrounding the power station. Any buildings that were here have been levelled to create a stretch of flat, arid wasteland. The second I spot the four famous chimneys, there's an ear-shattering screech and I crash to the ground with shock. Yelping with pain, I drag myself back into the shadows.

Rage is doubled over laughing. Pearse and Conall are smiling too. Dan-Dan is shaking his head and tutting gently.

'Jerks,' I snarl, getting to my knees and waiting for the ringing in my ears to fade.

'That place is packed with living, juicy humans,' Rage chortles. 'It'd be a beacon for every zombie within a five-kilometre radius if they didn't have a suitable deterrent in place.'

'It's like the system of high-pitched sirens around County Hall,' Pearse says.

'Only Dr Oystein told us theirs is far more

effective,' Conall adds. 'Lots more sirens and way more powerful than ours.'

'Nice of you to warn me,' I huff, staggering to my feet, almost back to normal, though there's still a pain in my teeth, similar to how they used to feel after a trip to the dentist.

'That's the price you pay for being an interloper,' Rage chuckles, then tosses me a pair of earplugs. 'They're heavy-duty. They'd block out the noise of a plane crash. Once you put them in, you won't be able to hear. We won't either.'

'That'll put us at a disadvantage, won't it?' I frown.

'Only for a while,' Rage says. 'The sirens are arranged in several rings, each attached to a separate generator to ensure they never lose the entire system at the same time. We figure they'll cut the last couple of loops as we get close, once they verify who we are, so that Owl Man can come down and chat with us.'

'We're all going up to the power station?'

'Yeah,' Rage says, shooting the other pair of Angels a dirty look. 'I wanted to take the Child Catcher by myself – the doc was in favour of that too – but these muppets insisted on accompanying me.'

'If we've come this far, we might as well see it through,' Pearse smiles.

'And what happens when we get to the front door?' I ask. 'Do we invite ourselves in for tea and biscuits?'

Rage scratches the back of his neck. 'We'll see how Owl Man wants to play it. We've discussed different scenarios with Dr Oystein, but ultimately it's Owl Man's call. We'll have to play along and try to make sure he can't pick us off too easily once the swap has been made.'

'You'll need to keep back,' Pearse says to me. 'In case the owl guy tries to turn you against us.'

'Nah,' Rage says. 'Better we stick together. She'll be a target by herself.'

Pearse shakes his head, lips pinched together behind the shade of his mesh mask. 'If you're willing to let her come with us, that's your call. But I'm not having her within easy striking distance of me.'

'Me neither,' Conall grunts. 'No offence, B.'

'None taken.' I cock an eyebrow at Rage.

'You should stay here,' he scowls. 'You'll be vulnerable in the open, cut off from the team. They might mistake you for a stray revived.'

'I can look after myself,' I tell him.

'OK,' he mutters sourly. 'If you're hell-bent on sticking your neck out, don't blame me if they chop off your head.' He crooks a finger at Dan-Dan. 'Here, little piggy. I'm gonna keep you nice and close on the way in.'

'Be careful not to scratch me,' Dan-Dan says as Rage pulls him in tight and lays a hand on his shoulder, fingers just a few centimetres from his exposed neck. I need to get myself into that position before we swap him, so that I can finish the job I came here to do. But for the moment I'll tag along, see how things play out.

'You'll be fine as long as I don't stumble,' Rage cackles. 'Right, are there any last-minute questions?'

'What do we do if they shoot B?' Conall asks.

'Nothing. Leave her to rot where she falls. It'll be her own fault for sticking her nose in where it's not wanted.'

'And if they shoot Conall or me?' Pearse asks.

'I'll have a mass said for you,' Rage snaps, then sighs. 'Look, this is a high-risk manoeuvre. They can't shoot me for fear I'd infect Dan-Dan. The rest of you will be fair game. If you cross that wasteland with me, there's a better than average chance that you won't be coming back. You should wait here. I'm the only one who needs to be present to negotiate. The rest of you will have nothing to do, at least until we find out how the swap is going to be handled.'

'You're not leaving me behind,' I bark. 'I'm coming no matter what.'

'I wouldn't have it any other way,' he rumbles. 'What about you guys? Do you want to wait for us here or are you as dumb as this stubborn bitch?'

Pearse and Conall share a worried look. Then Pearse rolls his eyes. 'If B's going along, we have to go too.'

'Yeah,' Conall agrees. 'We can't have a girl showing more balls than us.'

'What a pair of modern-day knights,' I laugh.

'Right,' Rage says again, angry but resigned. 'If

you're all determined to be a pack of martyrs, let's stick in the plugs. We'll take them out when we get to the wall. Until then, it's silent mode.'

I insert the earplugs. They're wax and I carefully prod them about until they fill the space entirely, blocking out all sounds. It's not easy because of the bones sticking out of my fingers, but I manage and the world becomes an eerie, hushed place. Seconds later Rage looks round and we all give him the thumbs up. His mouth opens and closes – he must be shouting to test the plugs – but nobody reacts except for Dan-Dan, who winces and covers his ears with his hands.

Rage checks with us again, then nods, takes firm hold of his hostage and moves forward into the open zone. The rest of us follow and take our first steps of the deadly march across no man's land, where we're easy prey for any snipers who might be keen to put a bullet or two through our undead brains.

NINETEEN

I've seen the landmark brick building from the distance before, but never up close. It's massive — makes me feel like an ant. We approach from the east side. There's a smaller, newer building attached to it here, and several entrances. Most have been bricked up, but a couple are in working order, barred by sturdy steel gates.

I can't see any signs of life. I suppose, even with the zombie-repelling sirens, the residents prefer to keep a low profile, so as not to offer their brain-hungry enemies any incentive to gather and attack.

A few corpses are scattered around the wasteland. All have been shot through the head, evidence that while we might not be able to see anyone inside the power station, they must be able to see us. I feel wretchedly exposed. I have to force myself to push on at the same slow pace as the others, several metres removed from them, all on my own, with no place to shelter if the snipers open fire.

Even with the earplugs there's an unpleasant hum from the sirens. My teeth feel like they're shaking in their sockets and there's a ball of white-hot pain building at the back of my eyes. I want to be sick, but there's nothing inside my stomach to throw up.

Trying to distract myself, I wonder how the corpses we're passing made it this far. Maybe they were deaf and naturally immune to the invisible barrier of the sirens. That seems like the most logical answer until I peer more closely at one of the rotting carcasses and spot a stream of dried blood and gunk on its cheek, running from its ear. At first I'm confused. Then I realise that these zombies were so desperate that they must have pierced their own

eardrums and deafened themselves in order to advance.

I stare at the pitiful corpse and fight back an almost overwhelming wave of grief. I don't know why this should hit me so hard, but for a moment I can't move. I stand, swaying, obsessed by the stain on the corpse's cheek, thinking of all that we have lost and done to ourselves as a people.

Then I force myself to look away and continue. There's no time for pity. I'll save it for later. Not that there's probably going to be a later for me.

We're almost at the power station when the buzzing from the sirens dies away. We pause and look at one another. Rage starts to remove an earplug. He eases it halfway out, waits cautiously, then slides it free. He nods to show it's OK and we all take them out. I keep mine in the palm of my hand in case they turn the sirens on again.

'That wasn't so bad, was it?' Dan-Dan smiles.

'Speak for yourself,' Conall mutters, rubbing his jaw. 'I feel like someone's been scraping blackboards next to my head for the last twenty-four hours.'

'You guys did a good job with the sirens,' Rage compliments the human.

'Only the best for Dan-Dan and his chums,' Dan-Dan chuckles.

'A pity you weren't so well set up on the *Belfast*,' I goad him.

He shrugs. 'We weren't expecting an attack from the river, but we've learnt our lesson. The sirens circle the building here.'

I stare up at the towering brick wall of the power station. With my fingerbones I could scale it easily – we can dig into brick as if it was mud – but I'm sure I'd be shot before I got anywhere near the top.

'What now?' I ask Rage.

'Let's wait for them to send a welcoming party.' He doesn't look as edgy as the rest of us. He always was a cool customer. There's not much that shakes Rage.

Nothing happens for a few minutes. I start to edge closer to the others, feeling isolated, but Pearse spots me and goes, 'Nuh-uh.'

I scowl at him. 'What will you do to stop me?'

'Yell out that you're a threat to Dan-Dan,' he grins

wickedly. 'They'll fire so many bullets into you that there'll be nothing left but ash.'

'I was getting to like you,' I snarl, 'but I've gone right off you today.'

'That's a shame,' he sniffs.

A few more spine-tingling minutes pass. The hairs can't stand up on the back of my neck since I died, but even so it feels as if every one of them has stiffened to attention. I want to make a bolt for freedom. The tension is killing me, or would be if I hadn't already been killed.

Then the gate nearest us starts to swing open. They don't have a fast-release system like they had in New Kirkham, but I suppose they don't need one, given the effectiveness of the sirens.

I'm expecting the Ku Klux Klan, and quite a few Klanners do spill out, but there are also a lot of soldiers mixed in with them, which surprises me. I didn't think the army would grant its support to a pack of white supremacists. I suppose these might be rogue agents, but in that case why have they kept their uniforms?

The Klanners and soldiers spread out and train their rifles on us. They keep their distance, hugging the wall. I can't see the faces of the hooded creeps, but the soldiers look as nervous as I feel. They don't like being out here in the open.

'Hi, guys,' Dan-Dan booms. 'I'm home.'

Nobody responds. A few seconds later Owl Man appears, striding through the open entrance, Sakarias by his side. He's washed the dog since I last saw them. Its fur gleams, not a single bloodstain that I can see. It's panting softly and looks like a normal, huggable sheepdog.

Owl Man advances ahead of his troops, but stops well clear of us. He casts his gaze around and smiles. 'What an odd-looking posse,' he says, taking in our array of strange hats and heavy clothing.

'You're no fashion model yourself,' Pearse throws back.

Owl Man turns his attention to our hostage. 'Daniel,' he nods. 'I'm pleased to see you again.'

'Likewise,' Dan-Dan says. 'I'll be even more pleased when you give them the boy, so that we can be rid of them. I hope you're not planning any nasty surprises. I don't care about their friend. I just want to get to my room, so that I can relax, summon my darlings and forget all about this ordeal.'

'No need to worry,' Owl Man assures him. 'We have everything in hand.'

'Vinyl's OK?' I shout.

'We have taken excellent care of him,' Owl Man says.

'And the others? I want you to set them free too. You said you'd try. You gave me your word.'

'I remember,' Owl Man murmurs. 'I have already broached the subject with my colleagues and they are open to negotiation. This will be a stress-free procedure. First we need to agree a format for the swap. I'm sure you have some suggestions. I have a few ideas too. We'll discuss them out here until we're happy, then Vinyl will be fetched by our good friend Coley – maybe the rest of the New Kirkham gang too, depending on how things go – and the trade can be made.'

I squint at him from behind my sunglasses. I'm

always suspicious when things sound too good to be true. But Owl Man looks like he's on the level. Nobody's trying to sneak up behind us, and he hasn't sought to use me against the others.

'I must admit, I'm surprised to see you, Becky,' he says. 'After what happened in New Kirkham, I thought Dr Oystein would urge you to stay away from me.'

'He did. I ignored him.'

'Ever the rebel,' he chuckles. 'That's what I like about you. It doesn't even bother you that your comrades are wary of the threat you pose, that they have insisted on a gap between you.'

'That was my idea,' I lie. 'I won't let you set me against them.'

'You don't need to worry,' he says. 'There will be no treachery here today.'

'I wouldn't be so sure of that,' Rage says softly. Then, shocking everyone, both the living and the undead, he releases Dan-Dan, turns swiftly, makes a blade of his right hand and drives his bone-tipped fingers through the side of Conall's skull.

Conall falls without a word. I doubt he even saw the death blow coming.

Pearse screams and reaches out towards his collapsing friend. As he moves to catch Conall, Rage wraps an arm round Pearse's throat, then smashes a fist through the mesh of his beekeeping hat. Four or five quick blows, one after another, until he's punched through to the soft brain behind Pearse's face.

Pearse spasms. Rage releases him and steps away, shielding Dan-Dan from the revitalised's thrashing limbs and spurting blood.

'Careful, my Lord,' he says.

No more than a few seconds have passed, but it feels like the whole world has turned on its head. Nobody has had a chance to react. We're all gawping at Rage, mouths open, heads spinning.

'See?' Rage says with gloomy satisfaction, turning his gaze in my direction. 'I told you you'd regret it if you came with us.' Then he smiles twistedly. 'Go ahead, boys,' he roars at the soldiers and Klanners. 'Blow the bitch away!'

TWENTY

'Ignore that order!' Owl Man screeches before any-one can start shooting. He stares at Rage, bewildered, eyes even rounder than normal. 'What the hell is going on?'

'I'm switching sides,' Rage says smugly. 'Dan-Dan made me an offer I couldn't refuse.'

'I thought you weren't interested in my riches,' Dan-Dan gasps.

'Everyone has their price,' Rage says. 'I got inter-ested when you started talking about a villa on a private island. I can see myself enjoying a long retirement somewhere hot and sandy, with a bevy of servants to wait on me.'

'Oh, you bold, brilliant beast of a boy!' Dan-Dan whoops, clapping with delight. 'If you weren't so toxic, I'd kiss you.'

'You bastard,' I croak, staring with horror at the corpses of Pearse and Conall. The blood has soaked into the mesh of Pearse's hat. Conall has a surprised look on his face, as if he'd just been kicked in the balls by a bull.

'How long have you been planning it?' Dan-Dan asks, beaming at Rage with awe, as if he was a movie star.

'I began thinking about it on the way back from New Kirkham,' Rage says. 'I couldn't do anything to help you then – there were too many Angels around – so I bided my time.'

'They were our friends!' I scream.

A troubled look flickers across Rage's face. Then he shrugs. 'I didn't want to kill them. I tried convincing them to let me advance by myself. If they'd heeded my advice, I could have simply set Dan-Dan free and gone in with him, no need for any aggro. But they wanted to be heroes. You did too.'

'I'll kill you,' I vow hoarsely, taking a stride towards him.

'Stop right there,' Dan-Dan snaps.

'Make me, fat man.'

'If you insist,' he giggles and lifts a finger in the air. 'When I give the signal, start shooting, boys.'

'Wait, Becky,' Owl Man pleads. 'I was not expecting this. I had planned to return Vinyl to you, the others too, if possible. I'm as sickened as you are by this act of wanton betrayal.'

'Easy, Owly,' Rage mutters. 'You'll hurt my feelings.'

'But this is where we find ourselves,' Owl Man continues as if Rage hadn't spoken. 'One wrong move now and I will not be able to help you. Daniel, will you object if I set her free?'

'Too damn right I will,' he smirks. 'She's going nowhere.'

Owl Man sighs. 'In that case, we will take you into custody. I must ask you not to move.'

I feel my arms and legs stiffen. 'Don't do this,' I

moan. 'Please. I came to kill Dan-Dan. I knew I'd be killed too. I don't mind that. I've accepted my fate. But let me have a shot at him. *Please.*'

It's a ridiculous argument, but for some reason Owl Man hesitates.

'I've chosen my stand,' I say softly. 'I probably won't get to that child-killing demon in time, but let me die knowing I did my best to make a difference.'

'Oh, Becky,' Owl Man whispers. 'You have made such a difference already. You don't give yourself enough credit. And there is so much still that you could do. Change your mind, I implore you. This is not the time or place for you to fall.'

'You're wrong,' I tell him. 'This is the perfect spot. I picked it. Let me have it. I hate having to beg, but I'm doing it anyway.'

Owl Man looks down at Sakarias, as if the dog has all the answers. But his pet only wags its tail and barks hopefully, looking for a treat.

'Very well,' Owl Man decides. 'Your limbs are your own again. Do what you wish. I will not interfere. Have your moment of brave madness if you must.'

'You can't be serious!' Dan-Dan howls.

Owl Man shrugs. 'You will kill her anyway if I spare her.'

'Yes,' the Child Catcher thunders. 'In my time, on my terms.'

'No,' Owl Man snaps. 'I will not have her tortured at your hands. Let your men kill her cleanly and quickly, before she can rip into you. Otherwise I will demand her release and you and I will clash.'

Dan-Dan mutters something beneath his breath then pulls a face. 'Very well. Let her race against the bullets. See if I care.' He stands straight and sticks out his tongue. 'Come then, little girl. Come to Dan-Dan. Let's see what you're made of.'

'You'd better hope they don't miss, big boy,' I sneer, taking off my sunglasses and hat, setting them by my feet, leaving them behind to serve as a memorial until the wind blows them away. I square up to Dan-Dan and flex my fingers. I'm grinning. I'm about to die, but I don't care. At least I'm going in style.

'On the count of three, fellas,' I call to the

marksmen lined up against the wall. 'No cheating. One. Two. Thr –'

'Wait!' someone bellows, and one of the hooded creeps breaks rank and lurches towards me.

'What now?' Dan-Dan groans, rolling his eyes.

I don't know what the Klanner is playing at, but this is a sweet, unexpected distraction. I ready myself to make use of it.

'No, Becky!' the man roars.

I don't recognise his voice, which is muffled by the material of his hood, but I pause, disturbed by the fact that he knows my name. Is this one of Dr Oystein's spies? Mr Burke was working for him secretly in the underground bunker. Maybe this guy is part of our team and thinks he can get me off the hook. I'm sure he can't, but figure I might as well give him a few seconds to make his pitch. He's put his life on the line, blowing his cover like this, so he deserves a chance to have his say.

The Klanner comes to a halt a few steps short of me and stares, eyes wide behind the slits in his hood. He's panting hard.

'What's up, wacko?' I snicker.

'Ignore this lunatic,' Dan-Dan shouts. 'Shoot the pair of them.'

'No,' the man yells. 'You can't do this. Lower your weapons.'

Nobody obeys his order. Quite a few people laugh at him. But nobody fires either. They're all as curious as I am. Also, Dan-Dan still has his finger in the air. He doesn't really want them to shoot. He's only winding me up.

The Klanner curses, then says, 'All right, don't lower them, you sons of bitches, but don't shoot either.'

'Why?' Owl Man asks, but by the way he smiles, I know he's one step ahead of the rest of us. He's sussed what's going on, even if everybody else is in the dark.

'I can make her come quietly,' the guy in the hood promises.

'Dream on, racist,' I snort.

'I *can*,' he swears to Dan-Dan. 'Just give me a moment. She'll do what I tell her.'

'Not in a million years,' I huff, but I'm not as sure

as I was. If this is one of Dr Oystein's spies, maybe he has a plan to get me out of here. I'm ready to die today, but it'll be hard to ignore the temptation of rescue if it's dangled in front of me.

'Daniel?' Owl Man asks pleasantly, teasingly.

'Oh, go on then,' Dan-Dan scowls. 'But if he fails, I'll have him flogged and rolled in vinegar.'

'Becky,' Hood Guy mutters, turning back to face me. 'You need to stop, calm down and listen to me.'

'Why the hell should I?' I growl.

'Don't argue,' the man snaps. 'Just do what I bloody tell you.'

'*Why?*' I hiss, taking a step closer to him, shooting him evils.

'Because . . .' He groans, then fiddles with his hood and pulls it off. 'Because of this,' he says with a thin, worried smile as my eyes widen with shock.

I stare at him in silence, everybody else looking on uncertainly, wondering what the big deal is.

'Well?' the man says, laughing shakily. 'Aren't you going to say anything?'

I can only think of one response to that question.

One word echoes through my brain, which has become a furious whirlwind of images, memories and emotions. So, in a small, scared voice, I whisper it, hesitantly, as if it's the first word I've ever spoken. Which, many years ago, when I was a baby, it probably was.

TWENTY
-ONE

'*Dad?*'

To be continued . . .